SON OF THE SLOB

ARON BEAUREGARD

Copyright © 2021 Aron Beauregard

All rights reserved.

ISBN: 9798529468494

Cover & Interior Art by Anton Rosovsky

Stained Glass Art by Katherine Burns

Cover wrap design by Don Noble

Edited by Laura Wilkinson

Special Thanks to Mort Stone for Additional Revisions

WARNING
This book contains scenes and subject matter that are disgusting and disturbing, easily offended people are not the intended audience

JOIN MY MAGGOT MAILING LIST NOW FOR EXCLUSIVE OFFERS AND UPDATES BY EMAILING
AronBeauregardHorror@gmail.com

Maggot Press
Coventry, Rhode Island

WWW.EVILEXAMINED.COM

For my family.

May we all find peace someday.

"Just a stranger on a bus, tryin' to make his way home?"

- Joan Osbourne

RIPPING OFF THE SCAB

I was getting tired of looking at his face. Dr. Plankton's sunken eyes, long fingernails, ghostly complexion, and pointed nose made him almost vampiric in appearance. If there wasn't a mirror hanging on the wall a few yards away from us, displaying his reflection, I might've even seriously entertained the idea. I'd believe anything after what I've been through. Monsters are real, and they don't look quite like the supernatural depictions on the silver screen. They look just like you and me.

They live in houses, eat their dinner every night, drive cars, and at times, we relate to them. Or at least we think we do. They can have the same benevolent gawk in their pupils that I look at in my own while I get ready for work in the morning. And in my mind, that's far more frightening than anything Hollywood can conjure up.

"Vera, did you hear me?" Dr. Plankton asked, sounding a little more irritable than usual.

"Sorry," I replied half-heartedly. It was hard at times to keep paying attention to him. He was so damn boring. Having virtually no progress after nearly a year of his therapy sessions would lead an unbiased party to think that *I* should be the irritated one. "Where was I, Dr. Plankton? I lost my train of thought again."

Dr. Plankton let out a subtle huff—a real prick move for someone who's being paid to listen to you. Then he smacked the heavily subtracted lead of his pencil tip against the leather journal. His writing utensil was *almost* as dull as he was. I wasn't in the mood for his childish passive-aggressive tactics.

I don't think he was coming off like he was intentionally intimidating me, but still, sometimes, it feels that way. If he'd been listening for the past eleven months then he'd understand, after what I'd endured, there wasn't a thing on this Earth that was going to rattle me. Certainly not some delicate nerd in an itchy turtleneck sweater that shops at Bloomingdale's.

I'd stared the devil in the face and walked away looking just like him. I glanced into the mirror on the side of his office. The gorgeous dark cherry-colored wood helped my reflection pop out from the mahogany backdrop. Speaking of monsters, here I am. My morbid expression was just one of the many problems we hammered out with redundancy.

While my face had healed, and I still had the use of my eyes, I looked distorted; my skeletal outline filled with the bumpy pattern of punishment he'd left upon me. My skin was discolored and stretched like a cheap Halloween mask sitting in the discount bin. I look like hell. And for as long as my lungs pull in air, I will always look like hell.

"You were talking about your transition to The Lonely Bug. I'm sensing some resentment in your tone. It's okay to struggle with change, Vera, everyone does. The human race are creatures of habit. We are often comforted by routine."

"Sure," I replied, not really wanting to get into it any deeper with him.

"Well, what's wrong?"

I laughed inside. Fuck it, I'll say it, I'm paying for the time. "Well, where should I start? Hilton? Should we talk about the Hilton?"

"If you'd like."

"The hotel I worked at for years faithfully, YEARS, never so much as showed up late, never a guest complaint, I did nothing but clean their rooms twice as fast as anyone else and did it twice as good—"

"No one is questioning your ability, Vera. I'm sure they valued your skills."

"What better way to show their appreciation than by severing ties with their most loyal and tenured employee?"

"They had cutbacks, that particular Hilton is not exactly what it used to be. Have you driven by it lately?"

"That has nothing to do with it! It's my face! We've been over this and you fight me on it every time, but you weren't there! You didn't see the cheerful children start crying! The disgusted couples snickering behind closed doors! They complained—I saw the written complaints with my own eyes! So, they can say that it was layoffs, you can echo it, but I know the hard truth. And the truth is, people are ugly, even uglier than me."

Dr. Plankton erased something from his pad, then scribbled down a buffet of notes with his whittled wood. He allowed his readers to slide back down to the tip of his nose before looking back up. I could see him readying himself to say it again… it was almost as if he had to work himself up to the long-toothed lie.

"You're not ugly, Vera. You're just uniq—"

"Can you spare me the pity today? I don't need you to reaffirm every negative topic we broach, okay?"

Dr. Plankton didn't answer me, but I could tell he was irked. He didn't like it when I took control of the discussion. But as long as I'm here on my own dwindling nickel, he'd better find a way to accept it.

I took his silence as a small victory and continued, "So, is there resentment for Hilton? OF COURSE. But I know that doesn't change anything. I know I'm still going to wake up tomorrow and nothing will be different."

"What about The Lonely Bug?"

"Well, it's a dive motel that's dumb enough to name itself after an insect. The one thing people dread when sleeping outside of their own homes. And trust me, it's not false advertising."

I slid my hands through my hair; I wanted to pull it out just thinking about where I was and where I am. The downfall was nothing short of pathetic. "I mean, am I glad to have a job that can barely support us? Sure. Do I like cleaning up blood, syringes, and condoms? Scraping roach guts off the cheap paneling? Seeing seedy people peddle false hope to broken souls every day? It sucks. But at least, for the most part, they look past me. I'm of little importance. Just another mindless leg on the centipede."

Dr. Plankton jotted down a few more words, "Well, that's one optimistic aspect to take from it, at least you can kind of just do your job and then go home…"

I could see he was running out of positives and treading lightly. He knew right where we were headed. Was he trying to divert from it?

"Yeah, home. Where the real problems begin…" I uttered, also not exactly excited to talk about it.

"How is Daniel?"

"He's there."

"Still sleeping in separate rooms?"

"Yep."

"Is that what you want?" Dr. Plankton asked, raising the eraser to his mouth and nibbling on it.

I really had to think about it before answering. There was a part of me that enjoyed my solidarity. A part that yearned to avoid rehashing the irrational madness that came with the never-ending unnecessary arguments. You can't remake a decision. I can't change the past, and for that reason, I'm doomed. We're doomed.

Then there was the other part. The slice of my heart that his initials were carved into like an aging oak tree. The part that missed the tender look in his eyes that screamed 'I'll do anything for you.' The man that couldn't stand up from his wheelchair, but bent over backwards for me. He was an incredible person. What the fuck happened to us?

I asked myself the question, knowing the answer damn well. It was beaten into my mug and ingrained in every fiber of my being. But that answer was a Pandora's Box that I could do without. It was a rabbit hole that would eat me alive if I chose to go down it. Better to answer his question than rip open that garbage bag.

"I don't know."

"Okay, well, maybe that's something you can think about a little bit more. In fact, I think it would be good to discuss it openly. The only way the two of you are going to be able to move forward is if you confront it."

"What do you mean, discuss it openly?"

"I'd like Daniel to join us on Thursday. I know you've shot down the idea many times before, but I think it's imperative to your progress. You have to honestly ask yourself if you want things to get better. There's only so much the two of us can do together, there is only so far we can go without him. Do you understand?"

I tried to exhale the fluttering dread bouncing around my belly but it only agitated my bowels even more. I don't like admitting the geek is right, but he is. Daniel and I hardly spoke anymore. We didn't fight at least, but our exchanges were all short and in a very transactional manner. More like brother and sister than husband and wife.

"I'll ask him," I replied with a hushed delivery.

"Wonderful," he mumbled, looking down at his watch and then back up at me. "Well, it seems we're over. That was fast."

That was debatable, but I was in no mood to argue with

him. I just nodded my head politely and smiled. "Well, I guess I'll see you on Thursday then," I replied, not really knowing what else to say to the man.

"And, hopefully, Daniel will be with you. Goodnight."

"We'll see," I said, closing the wooden door with the frosted glass window behind me.

I didn't want to exchange goodnights with him because it wouldn't be a good night. It was never a good night. Not since before I chose to knock on the door of that house in the woods eight years ago.

***

When I arrived home, the lights were off, as usual. While I couldn't see what was in front of me, immediately, there were other cues that were undeniable as to what I was returning to. When the door opened, the pungent odor of garbage and neglect greeted me. The same stench that I had strived for so long to omit from my surroundings had returned with a vengeance.

I didn't want to turn the lights on and be faced with it, but after so long, it didn't even matter. I looked at the filthy streaks of brown that were painted over and surrounded the light switch to my side. I thought better of activating it and instead turned away from the switch, and also the idea of illuminating the human swamp altogether.

As my eyes adjusted to the darkness, the moldy food, heaps of junk mail, and unnecessary clutter overwhelmed me. A sickening soundtrack accompanied the rotten visual; the faint scratching of the many thriving vermin merrily making their way through the grime.

I was too exhausted, both mentally and physically, to clean it. I couldn't remember the last time Daniel felt motivated to do a damn thing besides polish off another pint of cheap whiskey and toss the empty bottle into the ever-growing mess that was our home. He just stayed in his room. I was living in a house of ghosts.

I stared to the right at his door, wishing it was different. Inside, I wanted to push my way through the door and kiss him like we used to. Just lay beside him and hold him. Then ask him if he remembered who we were.

But truthfully, neither of us were ready for that. Maybe Dr. Plankton was right though. Maybe Thursday's meeting could see us find our smiles again, or at the very least, put us on the path to.

Then there was the other door. The door beside his that, no matter how I looked at it, was the imprint of our downward spiral. The morbid memory of the dirty bastard that took everything from us. The vein of our stress and throbbing agony and cantankerousness.

As disturbed and demanding as Harold was, it wasn't his fault. He was the product of undoubtedly shit genetics—a child of rape with a lineage that sounded made up. When I fought Daniel to keep him, I didn't know why. There was just a feeling inside me, an instinct that pushed me to.

Every time I look at Harold or think about him, the question is there again. It seems insane looking back on it. When the investigation was finally complete, the authorities could only surmise what happened.

By the time they got out to The Slob's house of horrors, the fire had destroyed almost everything. The fire ate away the wickedness and destroyed my answers. It robbed me of closure. In the end, all that remained was just a massive pile of charred broken bones and question marks.

The best answer they could afford me was that they had no idea whose child I was carrying at the time. The ownership of the property I was imprisoned in tied back to a wealthy businessman named Steffen Saint-Pierre, who they later found beheaded in a shallow grave with some other men on his mansion grounds.

There was no record of the man that destroyed me. No way to elaborate on the insidious mystery that had enveloped my existence to the point of suffocation. Maybe that's why I kept Harold...

Not that I was certain he would be able to give me the answers that I quested for, but maybe deep down, I just couldn't let go of it. Or maybe I had just seen enough death for a dozen lifetimes and couldn't help but spare him.

I suppose the reason doesn't matter anymore. This is my life. This is our reality. The darkness harvested from that experience wormed its way inside me, both figuratively and literally. It festered there like a fat parasite drunk off sex and violence. There was no changing it. I'd given birth to Harold Harlow, but to Daniel and I, he was… The Son of The Slob.

THE LONELY BUG

When I arrived at The Lonely Bug in the morning, the hookers and pimps were just clearing out for the day to go and do whatever it is they did. I always assumed before I started working at the motel that the normally nocturnal nomads slept during the day. That they were tired from the prior night's promiscuous activities and indulgence. But I soon discovered the sad reality, which was that they usually didn't sleep at all. They're fueled by the chemical escapism that regularly pollutes their systems. Maybe they're right? Maybe escaping reality is the only sane thing to do...

I don't like thinking that way, but the way things seem to be going, I can at least understand it a little better. When I stepped into the office, Felix was grinning ear to ear and staring down at a lewd periodical. The rows of lard that insulated his enormous head flexed with delight.

Anywhere else but the dump I found myself in, that behavior would have been considered out of line. But the area was a reflection of the harshest of times—the clientele was disgusting, and the motel owner putting aside his trashbag-mag wasn't going to change the bold cruelty of the environment around us.

Felix's eyes always seemed to bulge naturally and he had strange spaces in between his teeth. It must have been some kind of birth defect, but when he got *really* excited, like he was currently, little streams of his nicotine-infused saliva slipped through those cracks. He was repulsive, but who was I to talk…

As his drool finished dolloping the smutty ink under his moist orifice, he looked up at me. He used his wrist to slide the transparent slime off his face and set the magazine down in front of him.

I nodded my head politely and tried to avoid the small talk. Having a conversation with Felix was never much fun. It was usually just his adolescent-like sexual perversion shining strong, or on his better days, unclever innuendo.

"You know, you're so much prettier than any of these fuckin' bimbos. These girls are all just sluts, but you're the real deal. You're so raw, just like real life," he grinned.

I said nothing to the Neanderthal as I wheeled out my cleaning cart from the back closet. When I approached the front door again, he continued.

"I know guys don't probably look at ya anymore, after what happened to your face, but I still think you're pretty."

I clenched my teeth, balled my fists, and bit my tongue, but how much longer could I hold it?

"Vera! Hey! I'm fuckin' talkin' to you! Or are you so stuck up that my compliments are too good for you?"

I snapped my head quickly and finally unhinged my jaw, "No, it's just, I'M FUCKING MARRIED, FELIX! We've been over this."

At least my marriage is still good for something these days, I thought to myself, looking down at my ring. It didn't quite sparkle anymore. The grime that once again encompassed every inch of my being had besmirched the once-proud trinket. It hadn't been cleaned in ages.

"That fuckin' limp-dick-cripple can't give you what you need. You need a real man, not some gimp in a wheelchair. Smarten up, Vera!" he yelled as I let the door close behind me.

The heartless words and abuse were nothing new. It used to get me all worked up, and I'd spend hours going back and forth with him, but over time, the barbs had lost their sting. Life was so pitiful that disrespect was no longer a concern to me. Everything just felt numb now.

I pushed my cleaning supplies up to the first room and knocked gently a few times. There was no answer, so I tried again. Oftentimes, the occupants are either too hungover or doped up to hear me, so I usually signaled twice before trying the handle.

Still receiving no response, I decided to proceed. The squeaky wood came open and the inescapable scent of the downtrodden doused me. My sense of smell still wasn't incredibly receptive, but where I lived and where I worked were so nastily unique, that I picked it up with redundancy.

The work smells weren't quite as daunting as the ones at home. While they shared certain phases of funk, The Lonely Bug was its own flavor of repulsive.

At home, it was rancid and rotten, here it was more of a chemical smell. I never knew how crack, PCP, and meth smelled before I started working at The Lonely Bug, but I'd gotten so much exposure that I could've probably given the dogs in the narcotics unit a run for their money.

I could immediately tell the person who last used the room was on angel dust. The scent was harsh and similar to sniffing a permanent marker. The chemicals often caused incidents of rage and even temporary insanity. The hole punched through the bathroom door was another telltale sign. The hole wasn't there yesterday, so someone had a hell of a night.

The cracked and overly burned glass pipe sat beside the telephone on the nightstand. An empty pack of Newport cigarettes was there with several bare baggies around and inside it, and the spread was accompanied by a plethora of drug paraphernalia. There were also several empty 40oz containers of various malt liquor strewn about. Some were partially filled and stunk of dehydrated piss. Using them as waste receptacles didn't make much sense with a bathroom just around the corner, but then again, there were many things that didn't make sense about the place. I was picking up the stale scent of the alcohol now intertwining with the potent burnt odor of the PCP—a match made in hell for almost anyone that set foot in this place.

After I bagged up all the filth on the nightstand, I peeled off the comforter and sheets from the bed. Whoever had stayed inside had decided to use the bed as a toilet as well. The dry, shriveled feces were statuesque in appearance, which thankfully seemed to keep the smell to a minimum.

I stripped the bed bare, discarding the linen tainted with defecation into the garbage, and sorted the rest of the soiled laundry into the wash basket. I gazed down in horror looking upon the naked mattress. I never got used to digesting it, no matter how much exposure I had.

How many lives were spawned on this foul cushion? How many had faded or been snuffed out? The stains remained no matter how you covered them. In many ways, it was like my face, except there was no proverbial sheet for me to shield myself with. No way to cover up my history. It would always be there for the world to see and point at.

The bed bug problem had risen to a new platform of putrid. In most hotels, you had to check the corners of the stripped bedding to locate them, but these were so beefy that they were on the verge of ripping at the seams, and they were so plentiful that the mattress's floral exterior looked like it was riddled with some revolting furniture fungus.

They'd grown careless and brazen—drunk off the gore of the heathens. Human darkness and degeneracy are a deep disease, and now it had transferred from the minds of the nomadic scummy patrons and found a means to corrupt the most intimate corners of the pests' minuscule minds.

Trying to get rid of the bugs was pointless. The real solution would have been getting rid of the people. Instead, I just left them to their evil empire; the ever-moving, blood-sucking mattress of macabre would wait for the next crimson nectar pouch to pass out and then gouge relentlessly. The sickness was cyclical. It was just how it had to be; it would never change.

As the thoughts of filth, insects, and waste littered my mind, I knew I was allowing it. It was quite sad how far down the spiral staircase I walked every day. Into the bowels of Beelzebub, only to let my mind's eye drift. Allocating escape, evading the inevitable, sifting through the bloody piles of mind-rotting minutiae. It was all a distraction. One big, pathetic distraction for what lay beyond the door. For what I had to face when I left this shithole and returned to my own.

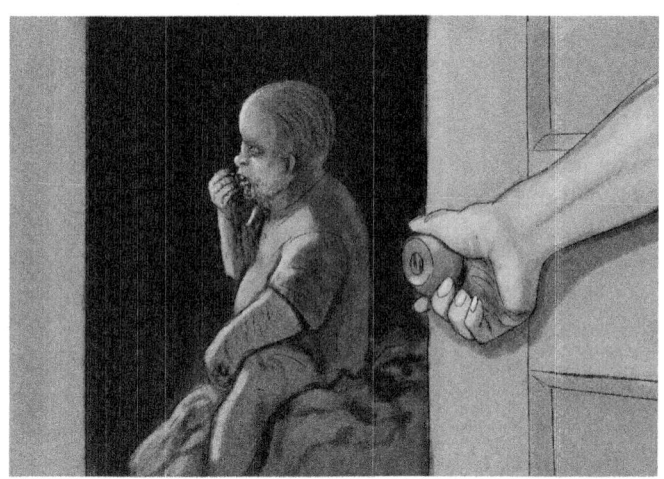

THE HUMAN LITTER

The cesspool of salty sin that was 'home' stood before me. Inside, I wished it didn't. I don't believe in parallel universes but I wish that I did. I wish this dreadful place could just magically disappear and I could wake up in someone else's skin. The version of me where things had gone as planned.

The once pristine conditions had all but wilted away; the only things that remained were the fear and uncertainty. The sour and moldy flavor of depression. The downright obscurity and utter madness that was a 'normal' evening in our strange hemisphere. I wasn't so blind that I couldn't remember, most times, I just tried not to.

What unspeakable horror would I find this time? Only my imagination could put a cap on it, and over time, with my mind constantly racing through a steaming buffet of awful outcomes, I knew the possibilities were endless.

I looked back at the sun setting each night before I entered, wondering how many more I would get to take in. What measure of mortality remained in the morbid snow globe that I was trapped inside of? It felt heavy and daunting when I estimated. Much of me had given up on the ludicrous happy endings I often fabricated in my mind. The fantasy could never manifest, the dream always mutated into a nightmare halfway through. How much longer can the pain go on? How bad can life get?

As I broke the threshold, the weight got heavier. My shoulders ached, my spine compressed, my intestines turned to worms; flailing inside like they'd been lit on fire. I had the feeling…

It's impossible to explain properly unless you've had it yourself. It borders on paranormal. You're immersed in whatever mundane task is at hand and, suddenly, all is wrong. The pit of your stomach is like a fucking jackhammer pumping wildly. It's like you need to puke but can't. You don't need someone to tell you that something horrific has happened, there isn't a doubt in the world. It's the same feeling I got the morning when my sister, Lisa, shot herself in the head.

I can still see my sister's vessel; bulging eyeball volleyed out of her skull, winking at me while jammed in the grimy heating vent. The darkness in her skull splattered all over. While her soul had finally escaped to go wherever souls go, her pulpy, corrupted cranium was left behind.

It was for me to deal with, for me to scrub into oblivion. In a way, it was sad. Lisa and I had our issues, but erasing the final physical traces of your only sibling is a melancholic conclusion that will never leave you. Once Lisa was dead, the feeling was all that she left. The wicked enlightenment that a profound dread is always in the background, lying in wait and ready to suffocate you at a moment's notice.

After you've tasted it, you can't forget it. You can't shake it. It stays with you. It becomes you. Because you know it's always lurking, and at any moment, the morose antenna can raise itself and point toward the patch of plantation where the next grave will be dug.

The sick thing is, I don't even fear the feeling anymore. I couldn't be bothered. I've been completely desensitized. The truth is, I'm so twisted up that my own instincts can no longer be trusted. Because I digest that feeling ritualistically. Like the hypnotic pounding of the drumskin by a follower, it was consistent—as dependable as rain on a shitty morning. Because every day is the worst day ever.

The gyrating gut worms reached their pinnacle as I looked at Daniel's closed bedroom door and quickly moved to the one beside it. A slice of orange light leaked through Harold's cracked door. It was calling me.

I could hear a rustling noise close to me; it sounded different than the vermin sifting through the garbage piles in search of a fermented snack. It was spilling out from Harold's room. It was coming right at me.

I crept up to the door and gently nestled my body against the framework, diligent in doing it silently and remaining unnoticed. His state of being required the snooping—my son had issues that needed to be closely monitored. It feels wrong saying it, but I've accepted that he's different. I had no other choice. His deformities leave him a far cry from normalcy and a distant scream from sensible. I've accepted that, at times, I'll need to study Harold anonymously like a zoologist would an exotic species of animal.

When I peered into his room, I saw his oversized face and blubber-insulated neck. It was eerily backlit, leaving a shroud of darkness covering his facial features. His glowing yellow eyes twinkled with mischief as the cloudy bulb of the nightlight reflected off of them. His obesity was disturbing; a child that was merely seven years old but looked about the age of a sixth-grader.

Every time I laid eyes on Harold, I was reminded of how unsightly his appearance was. He was the definition of abnormal. The poor child's hair was brown and medium length but he was born balding, like he'd exited my womb in the clutches of a mid-life crisis.

While hair was missing from his skull (amid other taken-for-granted, factory-installed faculties) in a cruel genetic joke, it had decided to sprout from other areas. His face had a five-o'clock shadow that could get served at any watering-hole, had it not been sitting on his morbidly obese but still obviously adolescent frame. The whimsical puberty push gave him a freak show quality, but not more than the follicles that were growing through the strange tops of both of his hands. The ape-like feature only further justified the animal correlation, not to mention his current action…

As Harold's wide waist and beefy rump sat on the soiled shag rug, I didn't want to watch, but I knew that I had to. He shouldn't have required diapers at the age of seven, but he did. He shouldn't have his diaper off, and a nutty line of bodily fudge caked against his bare backside, but he did. He shouldn't have the diaper sitting on the ground in front of him and the warm murky excrement compressing between his palms, but he did.

The consistency of the fecal matter was too lax to be molded into whatever construction his unsound mind had conjured. Instead, the activity just made him look like some kind of deranged savage that was playing in the mud. I didn't notice the brown traces that rimmed his oversized lips initially. I didn't realize what that meant until he scooped up as much as he could with those hairy paws of his, and unhinged his jaws.

The gunky exit material invaded his mandible to the point of overflow. As he chewed on the near-liquid form pointlessly, some of the excess squirted out, escaping his lips. I knew what it smelled like, the boy's scent of relief was potent enough to make me lightheaded, so I couldn't imagine how he might orally ingest such a foulness.

Juicy teardrops dripped down from my face while the sickly diarrhea ran off of Harold's. I had to look away from it. The thought struck my brain like a hammer on a bell. The abomination sitting before me was my son. A soul stuck in a bastard version of life that wasn't compatible with societal standards. I mustered up the courage and squared my watery vision on him once again. I needed to watch it, but I didn't feel compelled to stop it. It would only serve as a Band-Aid.

I wiped the salted water away using the back of my shaking hand. In the pits of his pupils sat obscurity—a blank slate that could only be brought to life by decades of brain-frying electroshock.

Harold swallowed the entire mouthful before he looked at me and smiled. He brandished another one of his more unfathomable features. The mysterious defect baffled any doctor I'd broached the topic with. Harold's teeth were as black as freshly laid tar and as yellow as the center lines that separated the lanes; he was born with rotten teeth.

Harold finally noticed I was there, but I was too upset to reprimand him. My spirit was too broken, how could I lead him when I couldn't even lead myself? Furthermore, Harold wasn't capable of receiving the message, of correcting the obvious error of his ways. He just sat there gleefully and reached for another handful of feces, just as I reached for the sticky door handle to pull it shut.

THE BABYSITTER'S CLUB

Thursday is my day off. I'd spent most of it lying in bed, listening to the sound of low fuzz on a snowy television screen, the patter of rain, and scratchy clawing of the vermin frolicking around the house. Mustering the willpower to trot over to the toilet seemed impossible, but eventually, I rose from my stagnant mattress like the dead.

The gloomy day gave me soaring anxiety for a multitude of reasons. Daniel had still not indicated whether he would accept my invitation to meet with Dr. Plankton, so the thought of how the day was set to play out was still looming.

With conversation being about as rare as winning a scratch ticket, I'd come up with another way to inquire. I'd delivered a rather juvenile note along with his dinner the prior evening. I wasn't sure it would work, but it was the only thing I could think of.

The half-frozen fish fillet, greasy French fries, and sloppy mash of mayo and relish all cornered the paper on the tray. When I handed it to him, he didn't have any reaction. Did he think it was a napkin?

Hopefully not, but at the moment, it seemed quite possible. But as I lethargically reached the grime-stained door, I realized the same slip of paper from the tray had been slid underneath the entrance to my room.

At first, when I saw the peppering of girthy mouse droppings that the parchment cradled, I wondered if it was merely another piece of trash in our landfill. Being always surrounded by garbage, it wasn't far-fetched to believe that could be the case. But as I squatted down, I could tell it wasn't—the turds were fresh!

The note I'd written him was straight out of middle school and included option checkboxes of both 'NO' and 'YES.' Daniel selected the latter. Just the visual of a shaky checkmark added by his trembling hand and occupying the uneven square made my stomach rumble.

I guess it's a good thing I found a babysitter in advance, I thought. I needed to believe Daniel wanted things to get better. I needed to believe in the positivity, and hope for the future, but there was no way to be sure. Now, I'm sure.

I exited my room and maneuvered my way around the piles of junk that surrounded the kitchen table. Finally, I set the note down amid the collection of junk mail and crusty dishes heaped up on our eating space. The next anxiety smacked me in the face before I could even begin to deal with the concept of the forthcoming therapy session with my husband.

I hope Harold doesn't react to the new sitter like all the others. Just this once. If he could be different, just this once, it would do so much for us, my jittery voice echoed through my skull.

There weren't many occasions that we required a sitter anymore. In years past, when Daniel and I tried to rekindle our love via a dinner on the town or taking in a new picture at the theaters, it always went horribly wrong. There were few victories in the familial war that was unending.

We'd spent most of those evenings chatting quietly. I watched as he tried to contort the loathsome ideas in his head. The ones that circled around his cranium to no end with the flashing speed of a shark in a swimming pool. The detestation that he harbored rent-free for me, but more specifically, the hatred accrued as a result of my decision to give birth to Harold. It consumed him. It changed him. The sweet and kind man in the wheelchair that had stolen my heart was now a bag of withering bones and odium.

Each night was capped off by a meeting at the residence of a tearful and traumatized sitter. The conversations were laced with outrage and disgust. The first time we met a sitter was also always the last.

The past sitters and their horrified banter were still fresh in my mind when I looked up at the fridge and stared at the ad I clipped from the Sunday journal of Harold's next potential victim. 'Why didn't you tell me he was like this! I never would have agreed to this!' The snot bubbling out of her nose between her salty eyes was unforgettable.

Was it really that bad? Am I just completely desensitized to the poor excuse for existence we've come to know? What is normal?

The few sitters we'd tried never mentioned exactly what Harold had been up to during their hours alone together. We arrived to most of them window watching, typically a crippling fright corrupted their bloodshot eyes. And then before we could even reach their doorways, Harold was outside, accompanied by the flurry of harsh curses spouted off by his temporary guardian.

"GET THIS FUCKING MONSTER AWAY FROM ME! YOU PEOPLE ARE SICK! HOW COULD YOU!" Those were just a few that I could recall.

The mystery haunted me to no end. *What was he doing in there?* I could only imagine. Whatever it was, they were too embarrassed to explain it. We hadn't obtained the services of a sitter in over a year. With the deafening silence that now encompassed our family, there was no reason to.

As I looked at the clipping that read, 'Eve Barron: Professional Babysitter,' my heart sank deep down into the pit of my stomach. Was this to have the same redundant conclusion as all the others? Would she join Harold's babysitter's club? Was I being selfish?

Maybe I was, but regardless of the outcome, Daniel and I needed to talk. We couldn't do it by ourselves. We needed help, and if that help came at the cost of Eve Barron having one dreadful night, I would just have to find a way to live with it. It shouldn't be hard—I was already living with a whole lot worse. I had nothing left to lose.

***

Harold sat playfully in the tub that was loaded full of warm and sudsy water. The build-up of soap scum around the moldy wash space held an uncanny resemblance to the unusual plaque that was caked all around Harold's seedy teeth. He'd lost a few already and I was hoping that his adult teeth would be different, but that wasn't the case. They were just as dark and foul as the baby teeth from before.

The smell of his overfilled diaper sitting in the can beside me molested the clean soap scent that should have been circulating in the bathroom. He shat the bed nearly every night, and since he didn't have the capacity to wash himself, it always fell on me. The ritual was growing old, no matter how much I tried to show him, he just didn't get it.

In a weird way, I kind of enjoyed that time together. While the foundation of our relationship was built on stress, he acted differently when it was just the two of us. While his deformed cleft palate didn't allow him to speak properly or comfortably, I knew there were things he wanted to say.

When I gazed into his buttery oversized eyeballs, I knew he loved me. Despite his retardation, I knew he understood and appreciated all I had done for him. He knew that I saved him. Harold had no means of conveying it, but in my heart, it was a sure thing. If it wasn't for me, he'd be in the trash liner of an abortion clinic or shaking on the piss-stained floor of an asylum somewhere.

When both my mom and Lisa were alive, I never quite understood how she didn't give up. Lisa's acts of violence, mood swings, and general rage were far more difficult to corral than anything Harold had done. But slowly, after having a child, I'd begun to realize my mother's conundrum. Eventually, she must have reached the same conclusion that I did—family is family, no matter how fucked up.

As I cleaned his chubby, coarse face, I reregistered that he wasn't always so foul and bad. He wasn't some demon like Daniel thought him to be. In his own way, I believe he was trying. Trying to do what we needed him to. Trying to be what we needed him to be.

"Are you gonna be good for Eve tonight, sweetie? So me and Dad can talk? So we can make all this better again?" I wasn't surprised when he didn't respond. He did look up at me and smile, which I took as a good omen.

Somehow, I was finding a way to be positive. It seemed almost miraculous. It came out of nowhere, but it was a thing of pure beauty. Tonight could be a turning point; a moment to look back on where things got better, and we all took a step toward being a family. Or, it could be the polar opposite…

THE ROAD TO NOWHERE

My stomach couldn't seem to settle once we pulled away from Eve's house. Her residence sat calmly in a nice quiet neighborhood. I'd seen the look on her face when she got a look at Harold. He was anything but just another boy. I watched the twinkle in her eye that she opened the door with burn out, and the smile on her wrinkly face melt away. I was grateful that she didn't turn us away—the bad vibes didn't outweigh her professionalism.

When I spoke with her on the phone, I mentioned that Harold had some special needs, but I intentionally sidestepped the specifics. It would only be a few hours, she could handle him for a few hours, right?

While the eagerness that had initially encompassed her demeanor had dissipated, she was still prepared to do the job. But there was a slight whiff of betrayal in the air.

With Harold in the care of another, I tried to focus on the next task at hand. I tried to ready myself for whatever might be said in Dr. Plankton's office. I had time to think, but as I stared back at the vacant car seat where Harold had been sitting, it was difficult.

For Daniel and I, the solemn car ride was exactly like the majority of our interactions these days—silent. Daniel stared aloofly through the smears of bird shit on the passenger window. It looked nasty; like a bottle of Wite-Out had been drizzled over the transparent glass. A beautiful backdrop of country roadway sat beyond the divider. In a lot of ways, it was like a metaphor for our own lives. Something that was so pretty, now distorted and blurred by a gross goop.

I'm surprised that Daniel even agreed to come. The man can't bring himself to communicate with his partner in a closed and private setting, yet he accepted an invitation to sit in front of a shrink? Maybe he thinks Dr. Plankton would be on his side? Maybe he was looking for his gripes to be validated. Maybe he realized that wasn't going to happen as long as our exchanges remained exclusive.

Aside from a few quiet thank-yous when I assisted him with exiting the car to sit in his wheelchair and opening a door for him, that was all that was uttered.

By the time we sat down in front of Dr. Plankton, my heart rate was out of control. The dread of the old grievances resurfacing in my hollows felt gutting. I couldn't help but question if the entire thing was a mistake, the same thoughts that had caused me to decline Dr. Plankton's suggestion on so many other occasions blared. What did it matter though? One more regret to add to the overflowing cemetery of stark disappointments wasn't going to do much in the grand scheme of things.

Dr. Plankton was dressed as snooty and prudish as ever, but there was something about him that was different… a curl on the corner of his mouth that I'd never witnessed. It was so nonchalant that almost anyone would have probably missed it. For the first time in our countless sessions, he seemed mildly amused.

"Daniel, thank you so much for joining us today. My name is Dr. Plankton," he said, coming around his desk and shaking Daniel's hand. "It's something that I really think is going to be paramount to Vera's healing process, and I'm also hopeful that you will achieve something from our discussion as well," he continued.

Daniel nodded somberly at Dr. Plankton, causing him to shift his gaze over toward me.

"And, Vera, thank you so much for having the courage to bring us together."

"You're welcome," I replied, watching as he turned back around and again found the leather chair behind his desk.

"Now, the only way we can rebuild our social roadways is to work, similar to the construction workers that make our drives to work so… charming," he snickered.

Dr. Plankton lifted up his small pad and a black pen. He jotted down a few things, setting up his page before he decided to continue with his opening statement.

"We need to reconstruct the damaged areas so we are free to travel those paths securely and without the fear of peril. Some paths we take are more difficult than others… some are longer than others. So, it's truly imperative that we start small. Rebuilding the skeleton for these basic paths will allow us to become more comfortable in discussing insignificant things," he explained, removing his pen from the parchment under his hand.

"Once we have the ability to talk freely about those mundane matters, then we can branch out. We'll further reinforce those roads and also create brand new ones by escalating the content of our discussion. Eventually, we'll ensure that the two of you are comfortable communicating no matter what route you choose to embark on."

Both the analogy and description were good, but are we rebuilding a highway or a relationship? Pouring concrete and laying black tar were laborious activities, but mending and tending to the rancid gushing wounds that remained ingrained in our flesh was something else entirely.

"Vera has brought to my attention in prior sessions that there is a strain between the two of you, which creates a tremendous difficulty in your ability to communicate with each other," Dr. Plankton explained, making eye contact with Daniel.

"But before we introduce that topic and branch off, I'd like to go backwards. Before the inception of any of these issues. I'd like for each of you to think about that time for a moment. I'd like for each of you to tell me one thing that you remember about each other from the first month you met. Something that helped you connect."

There was an uncomfortable silence between us. It had been some time since we'd been prodded to think positively. I could tell by the look on Daniel's face that he felt just as weird about the request. Then, suddenly, he surprised me.

Daniel looked at me, suppressing the smile behind his lips just like when we'd first crossed paths at the wounded veteran's center. Then he fixed his sights on Dr. Plankton and asked, "What did the cannibal do after he dumped his girlfriend?"

Dr. Plankton looked a bit baffled to have the question directed at him, but he played along anyhow.

"What did he do?" he asked Daniel.

"He wiped his ass," Daniel replied, brandishing his stained toothy grin for the first time since I can remember.

I wasn't expecting Dr. Plankton to enjoy the joke, but even he let out a chuckle. "I'm assuming here, but I gather there is some kind of significance behind that joke?"

Daniel's lip started to tremble. He ran his hand through his shaggy hair as he mustered the words, "She told me that joke around the time we met. And that was—that was… the first time I laughed after I got paralyzed in Nam. She gave me my smile back."

I couldn't help but try to keep from breaking down with him. Not even five minutes into the session, and emotions were running high. At least they were the good emotions. At least they were telling of who we were as people.

"That's excellent. That's an incredible example, Daniel. Vera, would you be able to share a similar experience?" Dr. Plankton asked.

The pressure was on now, although it wasn't a difficult question when I actually thought about it. There were countless things that the man had done for me before we'd become broken. Before we'd lost our way.

I wanted to talk about the extravagant meals that he used to cook for me daily, or how he went out of his way to keep the house spotless while I worked. His chivalry was without end, his love was overflowing. But instead, I decided to go with a more physical connection.

I turned back to Daniel and said, "The night we watched Fatal Attraction… I'll just leave it at that. It's kind of personal, but Daniel knows what I mean."

The nostalgia and forlorn joy of the old times was still lingering on Daniel's face from his answer. But in an unexpected mood shift, it quickly blistered and peeled off his expression. It was replaced by a seething resentment, by the exact display of antipathy that seemed to be all he knew during our dark period.

I was confused as to why that would upset him. On the evening we'd watched that VHS, we made love so many times. I'd never been so fulfilled, so smitten with anyone before. Why was he upset?

Dr. Plankton scribbled a few words down in his pad. Then he looked back up at Daniel, meeting his state of colorfully illustrated disdain. "Daniel? I gather, based on your reaction and mannerisms, that you don't see this event in the same light? Can you explain why?"

I felt the hot natural blush rushing to my cheeks; I hadn't intended to dissect our sexual episodes. But I'd opened the door to the conversation. I was at his mercy.

"She should know why," Daniel mumbled, buying time to corral his emotions.

"And she might, but if it's alright, I'd like to talk to you about it and just have her listen. Are you good with that?"

Daniel nodded, and the long hair dangling from the sides of his head that surrounded his overgrown beard rocked back and forth.

"Whenever you're ready, I will be," Dr. Plankton offered as gently as possible.

"She wasn't wrong," Daniel explained, sniffing up some of the runny liquid snot in his nostrils. "That was one of the best nights of my life too. I was given everything that evening. Things I never thought a mentally damaged cripple like me could dream of. I found my soulmate… I found my future… I found true love… and I planted my seed…"

Suddenly, it struck me like a ton of bricks upside my deformed head—our baby. I should have known he'd connect the dots in that direction. What we'd lost afterward was all he could think about. It was all tied back to the child that we were supposed to have together.

The blessing that was in my belly when I walked into that house eight years ago, innocently selling vacuum cleaners. The one that The Slob turned into golosh and fed back to me. The one that he sucked up any remaining remnant of and left fluttering in the red water at the base of the Bissell SC 1632. The one that would eventually be replaced with the Son of The Slob…

"Daniel, I didn't—"

"Vera, please, it's important that we let Daniel speak. You will definitely have your chance, but let's just allow him to put his full thought out, please," Dr. Plankton interjected, politely giving the platform back to Daniel.

He locked eyes with him, "Daniel, please, continue."

"Not much else to say, Doc. You know the rest of the story, don't you?" Daniel replied.

"I'd like to hear it from you… if you don't mind, that is. Perspective can be very telling and help us learn new routes to a potential resolution."

"It's all quite ridiculous," Daniel said as his hands began

to tremble uncontrollably. He slipped his arm into the side pouch of his wheelchair.

Daniel extracted what was supposed to be a stainless-steel flask, yet somehow, now, defying the marketing, it was grimy to the touch. A moderately-sized cockroach spilled onto the floor beside him and scurried under Dr. Plankton's fancy desk.

It was moments like this that allowed haunting thoughts to circulate in my skull when I was coming of age—*what if he finds the bug?! He'll think we're disgusting! We'll be shamed and embarrassed to no end!* But maybe that was the problem. I'd lost that fear, I'd lost my standards. I just simply couldn't be bothered anymore...

"Do you mind? I'll need a little to get through this, I'm getting the shakes. Ain't had a sip all day," Daniel said.

Before Dr. Plankton could say, "I'd rather you not..." the metal was touching Daniel's lips. The room-temperature whiskey nipped his tastebuds and woke him up. It put him back in the moment, back in hell.

"Well, I don't know what she's told you," he said, taking a second sip. "But it ain't pretty."

As the word 'pretty' flowed from my husband's lips, I looked at the mirror behind him, just as I'd done in Dr. Plankton's office many times before. Pretty was lost, it was something that I almost didn't remember having. Even though I wished each time I looked into the mirror, my misshapen mug wouldn't be staring back, I couldn't quite remember who I'd been.

It felt like a past life. Maybe that's why the garbage was swallowing us up at home, and why the filth fogged up any reflective surface. Maybe it was my coping mechanism? Burying the photos of better times and obscuring the horror show that I'd become was the safest way to keep my psyche insulated and forgetful. To protect me from remembering all that I had before it got flushed down the fucking toilet.

"If you could please stop drinking, Daniel. I-I just don't want to shift the focus of our discussion," Dr. Plankton asked with an admirable politeness.

"No prob, Doc," Daniel replied, quickly downing the remaining fluid in the tin.

He hardly winced and dropped the empty flask back into the creepy pocket of his wheelchair. I could tell that he needed that drink to take the edge off, but I was glad he'd finally finished up.

"Thank you, Daniel. Now, please continue," he said.

"Where do I begin?"

"At the beginning."

"Well, I suppose it all starts with that fat, hungover door-to-door salesman. That piece of shit brought the perfect storm to us. He came around with his fuckin' vacuum, trying to impress us. And she bit. She bit hook, line, and sinker," he explained, sticking his grubby thumb in my direction.

"You know my history," I interrupted, trying to defend myself.

"Vera, you'll get your turn," Dr. Plankton said, shutting me down once again.

"Next thing you know, she's at every doorstep in the state selling these things. Sure, the money was good, she was right about that, but I told her, ain't no reason for you to be selling door-to-door while you're pregnant. But one week turned into two, and a promising future turned into a nightmare. Turned us into people that need a fuckin' shrink to get by. How fuckin' sad is that?" Daniel asked, slurring his words slightly but still making clear points.

"You're not alone, many people seek counseling, and it's for a variety of reasons. You've both been through a traumatic experience. It's normal to feel shame in seeking out help, but it's not justified. You both deserve to find peace. It isn't your fault that this situation has been thrust upon you, is it, Daniel?"

"Certainly not *my* fault," Daniel replied, shooting a glare over toward me.

I found myself unable to hold back; dining on the rage that normally sat religiously on Daniel's plate. "Not your fault?! You could've sold the damn Road Runner! Then I wouldn't have needed to search and find creative income!"

"Bullshit! I told you to stop! We never needed that much money!" Daniel fired back.

"I wanted to give our baby the things we didn't have, the life that it deserved!" I screamed.

"Yeah! Well, how'd that work out for you?!" he yelled as the froth spilled off of his lips.

I broke down. The tears rushed out of me, eager to escape my monstrous vessel. Oh, how things had changed; we'd gone from blaming ourselves to pointing the finger at each other. There was no hope left in my heart.

"Daniel, Vera, please, just relax for a moment. We can talk about what we believe the root causes are, but we need to do it with civility," Dr. Plankton said, coming around the desk and setting a box of tissues beside me.

I drew two from the box and tried to compose myself. We both remained silent until Dr. Plankton sat back down in his chair again.

"Now, I know this is incredibly difficult. I honestly can't imagine going through the trauma that you've both endured, but I'm going to ask you to refrain from arguing. It won't solve anything and only serves to stunt our progress. Just take a deep breath and calm down. And, Daniel, I'm going to ask you to please try and avoid placing blame as you explain the circumstances. But it's important you continue, it's important we understand how you view this series of unfortunate events."

Daniel exhaled with control, contorting his nasty emotions and pushing them down into the same carnal box that he stuffed them into normally. I could see the routine was nothing new for him.

"Then what happened?" Dr. Plankton asked.

"Then she went off route. She went down a dead-end and found a house implanted in obscurity. A house where she was beaten and raped by a savage monster. The same monster that took our baby away." He tried again to hold back the tears. "She was there long enough that he wormed his way inside her to create the thing that we live with now."

"You mean your son, Harold?" Dr. Plankton asked.

"He ain't my son, might've agreed to let him have my last name, but make no mistake about that, Doc, I have no son," Daniel replied coldly.

The words were bareboned truth, but as they say, the truth hurts. He'd said it to me before, but it didn't hurt any less. It wasn't Harold's fault; he didn't ask to be born.

"Why do you say that?"

"Because he's the child of the murderous rapist that ruined my life. Is that clear enough for you?"

"Yes, I can see you resent the situation, and I can understand why it could be… uncomfortable."

"You understand? Ha, you don't have a fuckin' clue."

"I think I see the crux of the matter. Vera has told me previously about her decision to keep the child… you, on the other hand, wanted a baby that connected the two of you. Sadly, Harold, through no fault of his own, only reopens your wounds and agony. He reminds you of everything that was taken away. You resent Vera for her decision to bring Harold into the world and can't understand the choice, is that fair to say?"

Daniel gritted his teeth and nodded his head.

Dr. Plankton had been taking pages of notes throughout the duration of our exchange. He finally set the pad down in front of him and looked past the top of his glasses directly at Daniel. "But, Daniel, you understand, it doesn't have to be that way, right?"

"What do you mean?"

"You're still a family, aren't you?"

Daniel chuckled to himself, wiping a patch of wet drool from his lips, "You call this a family?"

"Families come in all shapes and sizes. My father died at a young age, my stepfather, to this day, is still my best friend. He's the reason for my success. It wouldn't be easy, but why couldn't you step into that role yourself? Just because

Harold isn't your blood, doesn't mean that he can't be your son. You might end up having something even better than you ever could've imagined."

Daniel couldn't help but smile at the thought. In many ways, his life was a horror movie, but on some occasions, he felt it was a comedy. He took a deep breath and returned Dr. Plankton's gaze of gravity. He allowed the doctor's monumental idea, and the heartfelt sincerity that it would've deserved had it been feasible, to stew in his brain.

"Let me ask you a question now, Dr. Plankton. Have you ever met Harold Harlow?"

THE EVE OF EPIPHANY

Eve sat on the flora patterned sofa while Pinky and the Brain tried to dominate the world on the tube. Harold sat watching the screen mindlessly. Eve was just happy that their interactions had been minimal, the cartoon appeared to be occupying him. Seeing how the boy's bizarre features and general strangeness just instinctually unnerved her, she couldn't have hoped for a better evening.

Harold's stature alone was more domineering than most of the children she watched. His bulky yet childish frame was not something you saw every day. His odd early hairline recession and nightmarishly stained dentures left a feeling of fright nipping at Eve's ticker.

Poor boy, he's just special. Probably has a hell of a time in school. The world can be a cruel place, Eve thought, feeling guilty about her prior judgements around his appearance.

It might've been Harold's infatuation with rats that held his attention to the silly show in an almost spellbinding manner. They were constantly rustling around his house and bedroom. He always yearned to get his hands on them and feel their soft screeching bodies trying to worm their way away from him.

Eve took another calm sip of her tea and felt a tingle continue to twist around in her bowels. She'd had to use the bathroom for some time, but wasn't keen on leaving Harold to his own devices. But the urgency of the situation was reaching a fever pitch. At that moment, she no longer had a choice in the matter.

"Harold, honey, I'll be right back. I need to use the restroom. Just keep watching your show, and if you're hungry, I can fix you a snack once I'm done," Eve said.

Harold remained motionless—staring into the colorful airwaves, and in absolute awe of the moving pictures.

Eve figured that she wouldn't be getting much of a response; the boy hadn't said a single word since he'd arrived. He just sat in that same spot on the rug, completely engrossed in the childish entertainment.

She pulled herself up from her warm and cozy cushion and exited the doorway, disappearing from Harold's vantage point had he been looking at her.

Mere seconds after she'd left the room, Pinky and the Brain concluded. A commercial for corndogs appeared on the screen and Harold's brow crinkled. His fat gut rumbled as the commercial ended. Suddenly, a live action show starring a handful of happy children that Harold had no means of relating to graced the screen.

"Snnnack," he muttered, rising to his feet.

He looked around the room for something to quell his hunger, but there was nothing behind him. His eyes returned back to the television, and more specifically, to the fireplace to the left of it.

Up on the low sitting mantle sat a single jar. It looked much fancier than any cookie jar he'd seen on the TV or in real life. Directly behind it sat a large oil-painted portrait of Eve's aged grandmother, Beatrice Barron. And next to the stunning urn, incased in a much smaller glass frame, sat a memorial card that captured the sum of the many highlights of the kind woman's life.

The shining red jar called to him—he could only imagine the trove of various treats that it might hold. Harold stood up on his tippy-toes and wrapped his fingers around the morbid container, carefully pulling it down. He resumed his seat in front of the tube, ignoring the happenings, only focused on the reaper's receptacle.

When Harold twisted off the top of the urn and peered inside, he was greeted by the most unusual 'powdered cookies.' While the substance was not in the mold of the cookies he'd eaten, it was the same color. In his mind, it must've tasted just as good as the solidified versions.

He dropped his hairy hand down into the half-filled vase and used his crushing grip to capture a dusty hunk of Beatrice's burnt body. Harold dropped the entire mouthful of mourning sickness between his jaws. He coughed immediately, casting off little dirt clouds of the cremation out onto the couch and all over the rug.

Eventually, he salvaged enough spit to saturate and help partially congeal the grainy ashes. As he manipulated the gritty mixture in his mouth and ground it between his teeth, he found himself capable of swallowing. He used the pool of collected saliva and his tongue to flick back the sudsy snack and force it down his windpipe.

His expression remained stone-cold stoic to the point of zombification as he reached back into the urn for another wad of wilted woman. The next handful was heaping; so overly generous that the initial cough sent more of the dustpan delight ejecting outward.

The violent cough even sent muddy streaks of the spit-soaked mess free to splatter over the front of the television, obscuring the happy expressions of the many children that continued on unnoticed in the background.

Harold's eyes reddened as he gagged on the incinerated ashes. He inhaled some of the dry particles and felt them tickle the rear of his lungs. The coughing fit did little to stop him from consuming the remains. He gagged, and burped, and spat, and slurped, and vomited into his mouth. But on most of the attempts, he found a way to gulp it down.

The watery vomit that kept working its way up from his guts served to help soften the ashes and made them easier to consume. The mucky mouthful that would have left most with their head in the toilet bowl, was about as normal to Harold as roller-skating was to most kids his age.

As Harold continued to mash his enamel into the dehydrated corpse-sand, he dropped his mitt down into the urn once again. His flabby fingers churned through the contents like beach sand. He was as happy as could be… until he was suddenly interrupted.

The blood-curdling shriek of his babysitter emanated from the doorway and quickly filled the whole house. The high-pitch horror expelling from Eve's orifice couldn't have been more justified. As she watched Harold cough out tiny clouds of her dead grandmother and gnaw on her final traces, the terror and disgust in her tone only intensified.

Harold looked up from his seated position to meet her mortified gawk and grinned. His hornet-toned teeth were heavily caked in her revered guardian's ashes and bone bits, and slathered in Harold's imbecilic drool as it dribbled down his stubbly butt-chin. He couldn't understand what all the fuss was about.

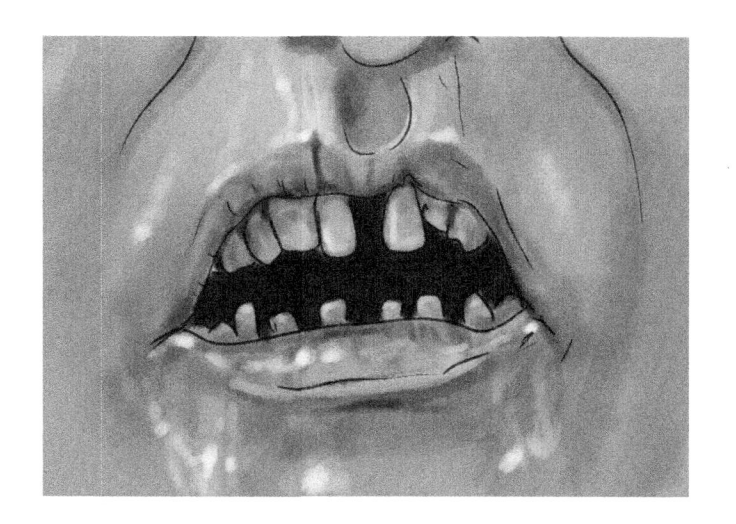

EXCUSES

The trip home was the manifestation of misery. Harold sat in the back seat, beside Daniel's wheelchair, gnashing his tongue wildly against his grimy gums. Aside from the faint vindictive wails of Alanis Morissette in the background, that was all I could hear the entire drive.

I glanced over out of the corner of my eye at Daniel. The gross action was wearing on me, I could only imagine that he was at a boiling point. He already hated Harold; it was difficult to imagine that initiating a new member into the babysitter's club had brought him closer to his heart.

What Harold had done inside Eve's house was unspeakable... there was no way around it, but should she really have left him alone? She's a professional, dealing with a special needs child, and she leaves him alone in the house? What did she expect? What did I expect?

As Alanis belted out her heartful hook, it was like she was directly answering me: "You, you, you, oughta know!" She was probably right. How did I expect anything less?

The evening was a total disaster. Daniel and I did little more than drive a fatter wedge between us in Dr. Plankton's office, and the terror in Eve's eyes when we arrived at the door was just another layer on the PTSD cake that was growing so high, it was fit for a wedding.

Harold isn't perfect, but he's my son. Part of me is inside of him. There is nothing that I want more than for those parts to shine through the darkness. To snuff out and overpower the warped genetics of his real father. But so far, it was clear that battle was being lost.

I had won a battle against his father once before, now he needed to do the same. It took me time to overcome it, you can't defeat an evil so profound overnight. I prayed that his soul would be able to do the same. It was my only hope...

But the signs weren't pointing toward positivity. They were pointing toward the same path of blackness that The Slob's obese footprints were stamped upon. But those were big shoes to fill, and this just seemed like an unintentional baby step in the wrong direction.

I looked back into the rearview mirror once again, adding a visual to the disgusting movements of his salivating food processor. It was hard not to be reminded of the horrific carnage I'd seen his father commit.

While I had hope, the facts were the facts. He'd already found a way to eat a dead woman before hitting puberty. Sure, he'd done so inadvertently; I don't see how Harold could've known what was inside that container. If he can't comprehend basic mathematics, he certainly doesn't know what an urn is. Yet, still, part of me wonders...

"WOULD YOU STOP THAT!" Daniel commanded, finding his first words of the drive.

The ask didn't seem to register with Harold, his chalky gums, gunky tongue, and ash-smeared lips continued to do mindless rounds.

"I SAID STOP IT! STOP IT!" Daniel screamed.

"Daniel, relax, I don't think he understands what you're asking him to do," I reasoned.

"He fuckin' knows! He knows exactly what he's doing!" Daniel retorted.

"I'll just—I'll just turn up the radio so you can't hear it," I replied, looking to defuse the situation.

As I reached for the knob, Daniel's hand shot up and grabbed me by the wrist. "No, he's gonna stop." His stern tone frightened me—I'd never heard him sound so cold.

Daniel flipped down the passenger mirror in front of him and looked back into Harold's yellow eyes. "Stop it now, Harold, or you're gonna regret it," he threatened.

The maddening strokes of the pooling spit swashing around his palette continued a few more revolutions. He was doing it even louder and faster than before.

"Son-of-a-bitch," Daniel muttered.

"He doesn't understand!" I yelled.

Daniel turned his body and sent a stiff backhand into Harold's mug with little to no reserve. The sickening mucky saliva splashed against the rear window and dribbled slowly down the side.

"You understand me now?!" Daniel wailed.

"Daniel! What the fuck are you doing?" I screamed, thrusting my own palm into the side of his cheek. "You don't hit my son! Do you hear me?! You don't put your hands on my fucking son!" I screeched, sending a second closed fist strike into the same spot.

My own outburst caught me off guard. It seemed to have also caught Daniel off guard. I gathered up my emotions and held them all in, just like I always did. In the decade-plus span that we'd known each other, never was there the faintest of foreshadowing that violence would transpire between us. With each moment that we continued to exist, it seemed like we found a way to reach new lows.

The silence that we'd grown so accustomed to returned. For the rest of the ride, Daniel stared out the window, looking like he was thinking about jumping through it. My mind told me that I should've wanted to cry, but it all just seemed normal now. Nothing could shock me anymore.

I wished I could be anywhere but in the driver's seat. In a way, it was a metaphor for our family dynamic. I was always the referee, I was always the peacemaker, I was the driving force. And now I was steering us into violence and mutiny.

As we trailed off down the dark suburban road, the bleakness of my existence grinded inside me. I fixed my eye into the rearview again to check on Harold. His rotten teeth had constructed a sinister grin that was painted with the red leaking down from his bloody nose.

THE SHORT BUS

I finished slipping on my uniform and peeked out of my room to see if Harold was still waiting by the door. I woke up with a brain of cobwebs—did last night really happen? How did things reach this sad stage?

I knew the answer to the questions, but couldn't help trying to conjure up different reasons. There were none. Where do we go from here? While last night was the only incident of abuse that had ever occurred, there was no indication that it might take a turn for the better.

I knew Daniel had probably gotten the message—striking Harold couldn't and wouldn't happen again. But was once too much? I'm not sure I'm in a position to decide… without Daniel's disability, we can't afford the mortgage. Regardless of what the circumstances are, and if our marriage can be mended, the reality is that we need to find a way to hold it together.

While the action Daniel took against Harold was stern and reprehensible, what Harold had done wasn't much better. The difference is, I believe Harold didn't know what he was doing was wrong. The situation was what it was—fucked. But I could only wait and see what would happen next, and deal with the trajectory as it unfolded.

The short bus was running a bit late, I noticed, stepping out of my bedroom and looking up at the dust-draped wall clock. Hopefully, it would be here soon. Otherwise, it could potentially have me running a little late for my cleaning schedule at The Lonely Bug. More than anything, I didn't want to hear Felix's big mouth, or give him ammunition to interact with me.

As I maneuvered my way around the heaps of rubbish, I listened to the rattle of our nasty housemates flutter through the dominant debris. I snatched up my purse from around the end of the chair in the dining room and pulled closer to the front door.

Standing a few feet behind Harold, I watched him linger idly with his Teenage Mutant Ninja Turtles lunchbox in hand, and JanSport book bag hanging off his back.

I'd wiped all the blood off his face and had him rinse his mouth out with Listerine the prior evening. He cleaned up better than I thought he would. Thankfully, Daniel's blow didn't leave a mark, despite bloodying him up.

As I stared at my expressionless child, all of his past cringe-worthy encounters with other sitters flashed through my mind. Almost any interaction he'd ever had with someone outside of our grungy house had ended in the same disgusting and disappointing fashion. Except when Harold was in school…

I decided to send Harold to a Catholic school more out of desperation than any kind of compelling belief. Saint Leo the Great Elementary School had a program that accepted mentally disabled children as pure charity. Which was the only way he would've been able to attend, because we had no ability to pay for a gouging tuition.

Whatever those nuns were doing seemed to work. Outside of one recent isolated incident, I'd never so much as heard a peep about behavioral issues since he'd started attending a few years back. I just continued to hope that the one-off detention he'd gotten didn't turn into a trend.

Education was one of the many backbreaking burdens that I had to help Harold navigate through. Knowing that he was in good hands and not causing a ruckus allowed an unnerving weight to be lifted from my shoulders. At least one thing was going right.

His grades weren't the best, and he was having trouble in many subjects, but so were many of the other special needs children. Sister Doomus had explained to me on a few different occasions that it was completely normal. It took more time for boys like Harold, but eventually, they always find their way. She assured me of that much.

Daniel had lost his faith in God during the war, but didn't much give a shit about any decision I made regarding Harold or his future. He couldn't be less involved. I'm honestly not even sure he was aware of exactly what school Harold was attending.

Not that I was a basket of belief either, but I still had a smidge of faith inside. I had to really; it was the lone hope that remained. There certainly wasn't any help for Harold that could be offered by the modern world. I searched for it tirelessly. He'd been to a variety of different youth counselors and therapy sessions. They all seemed to yield the same blank results. His interaction with them was non-existent. So, where else could I turn?

Maybe a more supernatural path was the only way. No one else could lend us a hand, so why not? The bottom line was, we desperately needed help, and asking God couldn't hurt. I figured he owed me one for the shit hand he'd tossed out onto the table in front of me.

I looked at my watch, beginning to sweat a little more, then simultaneously heard the drawn-out screech of brakes.

"Thank God," I whispered.

Harold turned back toward me slowly, "God?" he said.

"That's good, honey, you're learning." He drew the first and most likely the only smile of my day out. I kissed him gently on the head and ushered him out the door.

He took a few hesitant steps toward the bus and looked back in my direction.

"It's okay, sweetie, you can get on the bus now."

There was a strangeness woven into his glossy glare, I couldn't quite put my finger on what it attempted to telegraph to me.

"No need to worry, honey. Remember, God is always watching over you. If you get nervous at school, he'll always be there to help."

Harold stepped onto the bus and lethargically waddled down the aisle before finally working his bulky frame into the seat. The bus driver waved at me politely and then disappeared down the street.

AN EDUCATION IN EVIL

Sister Doomus was waiting at the bus stop for the special children to arrive. Her icy blue eyes glared at the short bus as it rolled closer to the weathered brick building beside the vintage church. Her short, prudish hairstyle was covered by her coif, and the surrounding veil and tail of her black habit garment danced in the nippy winds.

The dead leaves cycled in a spiral beside her as the short bus finally ceased movement. The door popped open and Harold, along with two other children, stepped onto the curb beside the towering nun.

A cheesy grin crinkled Sister Doomus's face. Her flabby cheeks puffed out more prominently as she pointed to the door ahead. "Let's go," she commanded.

Harold and the other children obeyed her direction. They formed a sloppy line as best they could, and with a hint of dejection, proceeded to file their way through the chipped wooden doors of Saint Leo's.

Once inside, they followed Sister Doomus down the dark hallway, passing the numerous classrooms that were already occupied by the paying patrons of the private school.

At the far end of the hallway, there was a staircase that led into the basement of the out-of-date building. The children followed Sister Doomus down the dirty pair of adjacent steps until they reached a black door at the bottom.

Once in front of the cobweb-cluttered doorway, Sister Doomus extracted an iron ring and inserted a slender rusted skeleton key into the hole just below the handle. She twisted it and the sound of the squeaky lock popping open traveled up the gloomy staircase.

She slowly opened the door, revealing a dreary learning environment that would have left almost any of the parents, had they been aware of the scandalous standard, filled with vehement outrage.

The corroded piping snaked across the dreary drop ceiling, and the discolored brick windowless walls boxed them in. The funky scent of mold and rust permeated the air, and unsanitary drips from the grey water piping that led to the girls' lavatory above them fell down into a filthy beige bucket beside Harold's desk.

There were six desks in total in the basement—only three of which were currently occupied. Harold crept to his desk and slung his book bag on the back of his chair, then set his turtle green lunchbox on the floor under his seat.

Shelly Trout took her seat to the left of Harold. She was nearly as obese as he was, but much tinier. Her body frame seemed to make more sense considering her age. They were both seven years old, but Harold was far larger in stature.

A purple headband rested above Shelly's puny eyes and shrunken face. There were also banana clips and scrunchies that were tangled inside her massive mane. She had plenty of hair to accommodate the extra accessories, but the choice to include so many seemed to border on obsessive.

The seat to Harold's right was the next to be filled. Benji Parker, a boy even smaller than Shelly but two years her elder, sat shaking his head from side to side and quietly snapping his fingers, then picking at his cuticles compulsively. His shimmering mushroom cut reflected the light given off by the single dangling bulb that hung a few feet behind them.

"Benji!" Sister Doomus yelped, smacking her beefy liver-spotted hand down on the bible that sat at her desk.

The confused boy froze in sheer terror mid-shake and quickly refocused his attention back toward the front of the classroom.

Sister Doomus picked a rosary off of her wooden desk and toyed with one of the unusually oversized black beads between her fingers. She closed her eyes and whispered, "Father, please give me the strength today," inaudibly under her breath.

After a few moments of mumbles, Sister Doomus opened her eyes once again. She looked over to Shelly and solemnly asked, "Would you mind starting us off with a morning prayer, my dear?"

Shelly nodded nervously and sat on her hands. She cleared her throat and began, "Our father, who aren't—"

"Silence, you mongoloid! That was a test! A test that, unsurprisingly, you have failed miserably. Not you or the rest of these heathens are worthy of prayer! You should know better!" Sister Doomus's tone was seething with hate and detestation.

"You have a long path to travel down before you are worthy of speaking to *my* God!"

"I'm sorry, Ms. Doomus!" Shelly cried.

"Silence! And it's Sister Doomus, you simpleton!" Each word she spoke had her shaking with wrath. After taking a deep breath, she calmed herself some and knocked down her tone a few notches.

"Now, while your apology is appreciated, Shelly, your

misstep cannot go unpunished. You must learn from this sin, you must find a way to comprehend it."

Sister Doomus eyed the brown drops that continued to trickle down from the waste pipe above them. "Take two drinks from the collection bucket, and say one Hail Mary in silence. And may the Lord forgive you of all your sins."

The all-encompassing dread paralyzed Shelly's face. She knew what had to be done, otherwise, she knew far worse cruelties would be on the horizon, but still, she remained.

"Ah, you wish to disobey me? Such a futile choice, but I'm not surprised, my dear," she replied, placing her rosary on the desk and reaching into the top drawer.

With one hand, she extracted a mucky platinum chalice. The sacrilegious cup was stained with past indiscretions of a guttural nature, and bedazzled with various multicolored jewels. In her other hand appeared a plastic baggie with hundreds of grains of uncooked rice.

Sister Doomus pulled the bucket along to the back of the room and set it atop one of the unoccupied desks. She set the chalice down right beside it and tore open the plastic baggie of raw rice. On the cold stone ground below, she spread the rice out until dozens of pieces sat on every square inch for a few feet.

Without speaking a word, Sister Doomus returned to Shelly's side and clasped her pruned fingers around her ear, then pulled. The pain of the flesh stretching out broke Shelly out of her fear stupor. She whined quietly under her breath as she was led up to the decaying wall.

"Kneel!" Sister Doomus commanded.

Shelly did as she was instructed to. Her bulky bare knees crept out from underneath her uniform and connected with the torturous grains. The pain was instantaneous and shot into her kneecaps like a bullet from a gun. The weight of her obesity only served to further annunciate the anguish and left tears streaking down her chubby cheeks.

"And now," Sister Doomus began, dipping the cup into the grey water, "you shall drink."

SON OF THE SLOB

"N-No—" Shelly pleaded.

"SILENCE!" Sister Doomus ordered once again.

As she dipped the unhygienic goblet into the raunchy waters, a variety of vileness flooded into the tin pit. The pungent odor of dehydrated urine dominated a concoction that also included excrement, blood, and water. There was a stomach rumbling thickness that saturated the collection. So much so that when Sister Doomus initially dipped into it, the metal rim of the chalice pierced through a filmy skin that had coagulated atop the fluid.

"Drink, my child, and all shall be forgiven," she said.

Shelly reluctantly opened her quivering mandible and allowed Sister Doomus to pour the contents of the ghastly bucket down her throat. When Shelly began to gag, Sister Doomus set the chalice on the desk and positioned herself behind the girl. She clasped one hand over her mouth and used the other to pinch her nose shut.

As Shelly's eyes reddened and her body tremored, she had no other option but to swallow. The oversized gulp traveled down her gullet, and she felt the gunky film from the top of the cesspool of bodily soup slime her esophagus on the way down.

Once Sister Doomus felt the mouthful run its course, she returned to the bucket to gather the second helping. She repeated the same sinister process on the helpless girl until the follow-up wave of vomitus mixture intermingled in her belly with the first.

"Excellent, now remain kneeling through your Hail Mary, then clean yourself off in the lavatory," she said, pointing to the girls' room that sat beside the boys' room, connected to the end of the teaching space.

She returned the bucket to where the drip still fell every minute or so, and grabbed the chalice and ripped plastic. She threw away the wrapping and placed the nasty cup back into the bottom drawer of her desk. She used a tissue to wipe her hands dry and then closed her eyes, commencing the morning prayer.

"Come, Holy Spirit, fill the hearts of Thy faithful, and kindle in them the fire of Thy love!" she hollered.

"Oh my God, I most humbly thank Thee for all the favors Thou hast bestowed upon me up to the present moment. Even the wretched ones that sit before us wreaking of wickedness. I give Thee thanks from the bottom of my heart that Thou hast created me after Thine own image and likeness, that Thou hast redeemed me by the precious blood of Thy dear Son, and that Thou hast preserved me and brought me safe to the beginning of another day. Brought me safe to guide the young sinners and corrected their blasphemous ways. To show them the light. I offer to Thee, O Lord, my whole being, and in particular, all my thoughts, words, actions, and sufferings of this day. If these lost simpletons could believe, they would, but they are not capable. So, I shall guide them, with your ideology, like the Lamb guided humanity. I consecrate them all to the glory of Thy name, beseeching Thee that through the infinite merits of Jesus Christ my Savior, they may all find acceptance in Thy sight. May Thy divine love animate them, and may they all tend to Thy greater glory... Amen."

Sister Doomus pulled herself out of the trance-like state that had possessed her. For a moment, it seemed as though she was trying to remember what came next. A light finally came on inside her.

"Alright, class, today we'll begin with math. I'd like you to take out your math books and turn to page fifty-four. Quite frankly, where we left off last time was pathetic. An utter disaster really. I hope you're extra motivated today because, if you're not, I've got some extra motivation in store that I plan to manufacture myself."

Harold and Benji watched Sister Doomus write the number '54' out on the chalkboard. Neither of them had been taught to count properly, so they were grateful she wrote it out. They just tried to match up what they saw to the corner of the book.

As they both unzipped their backpacks gravely and

extracted their textbooks, Shelly rose to her feet and began to brush the hard rice grains that were embedded into her enflamed kneecaps off to the ground. Once they'd been cleared, she quickly made her way to the lavatory as Sister Doomus had instructed her to.

"Now, the problem we left off on is at the top of the page. This is simple addition, and we should be far past this learning curve by now. So… HAROLD!"

Harold's body jiggled, slighted at the behest of Sister Doomus's unnecessary voice inflection. Nonetheless, his attention had been wholly captured.

"I'm going to give you the first opportunity to answer since it seems you're the furthest behind. A simple problem really," she explained, writing out '1 + 3 =' on the chalkboard.

"One plus three, what does it equal?" she asked.

Harold remained in eye contact with her but hadn't the faintest idea what she was asking him. He smiled and nodded his balding sweaty head lethargically, as if the gesture in itself was an appropriate answer.

"Nothing to say? What a surprise. Well, you're going to have to learn to be more talkative at some point, and you're going to have to learn your math. I have a feeling the Lord and I will find a way to get something out of you today… Shelly! Get out here!" Sister Doomus barked.

Shelly, still trying to control her tears, came barreling out of the bathroom. She stopped just short of her desk and asked, "Yes, Ms. Doomus?"

"IT'S SISTER DOOMUS!"

"I'm sorry!"

"Forget about that! Go and help Harold up to my desk," she ordered. Sister Doomus lifted the heavy textbook off of her desk and closed it slowly.

Shelly wandered dolefully over to Harold and explained, "Ms. Doo—" she quickly corrected herself, "Sister Doomus wanted, she… she wanted me to bring you up to her desk…"

Harold rose from his seat as requested, and Shelly held his hand while they approached the dirty wooden surface at the end of Sister Doomus's desk.

"Yes, step right up here, mister," she continued. "Nestle right up against the edge."

The unclean rickety writing table was nearly parallel with Harold's pelvis, which is exactly where Sister Doomus wanted him to be.

"It's time you learn how to add and communicate with others properly. Shelly, unzip his pants."

Shelly did as she was told. Due to the nature of Shelly's mental hindrances and how deeply the children were so entangled in obedience, there was no questioning the task.

Harold stared at Sister Doomus thoughtlessly. He had no guess or understanding as to where she was headed.

"Now, take his privates out."

Shelly giggled innocently and reached inside. There was a ridiculous weight under Harold's belt, one that wouldn't fit through the small hole in its totality, and one she couldn't really get to because of the warm and moist diaper that wrapped around him.

"It can't—it won't fit," Shelly replied, frightened at the thought of any potential response.

"Unbuckle his belt then, figure it out!"

Shelly did as she was told, and after a minute of struggle, Harold's pants had been undone and slithered their way down to his ankles. Shelly began to manipulate his diaper, and as she dragged it downward, a rancid smell molested the moldy learning space.

"Oh heavens! Lord!" Sister Doomus mumbled turning her head in disgust.

"I think he did a dookie!" Shelly yelled, pointing and glaring at the dehydrated fecal matter that had convened at the bottom of Harold's Huggies.

"Silence!" Sister Doomus commanded. Her eyes closed momentarily before reopening and focusing on the newly uncovered bulge that Harold housed.

SON OF THE SLOB

"My word..." Sister Doomus remarked.

The enormity of his scrotum was unfathomable. Without even considering the boy's age, even attached to a man, nothing Sister Doomus had ever envisioned could be comparable. The stretchy skin sack was elasticized to the creator's capacity. One more millimeter of testicle and the surrounding filling would have torn the skin at the seams.

Harold, like his father, was all balls. Not that his manhood should have been impressive at his age, but it was as dainty as a dandelion. Inverted into itself, the prick sat pathetically, just like the individual it was attached to.

"Put it on the desk, Shelly," Sister Doomus instructed.

Shelly used both hands to lift the hyper-tightened cluster of elephantiasis up onto the splintery desktop.

"Now, I'm going to show you how many one is," she explained, pointing back to the chalkboard behind her.

Sister Doomus lifted up the heavy hardback textbook until it was several feet above where Harold's testicles rested on the desk. "One," she called out, allowing her grip to fail.

The thick math book came down spine-first, smacking his testes with the full gravitational force. When the book connected, it caused the jelly sack to jiggle and scrape against the splintery wood beneath it.

"Aurghhhuu!" Harold bellowed out with an inhuman tinge now molesting his tone.

"Don't you move a muscle, mister!" she said, lifting the book up again. "And this is two!"

It descended at freefall speed again, smashing down into Harold's flesh basket and garnering another horrified whimper.

"And this is three!"

When the book connected the third time, the chafing skin was partially penetrated by a thin but painful splinter.

"And this, of course, is four!"

"Ahhhhhaaaaaruu!" Harold muttered, keeping his pitch inside despite the pain. The final drop helped the wood fragment disappear in its entirety inside Harold's ballbag.

The hurt was so intense that it caused Harold to jerk his burly bundle off of the desk, snapping the base of the splinter.

"I told you not to move!" Sister Doomus cried.

Suddenly, a thunderous knock rapped harshly against the grimy wooden door.

"Back to your desks! And you, go on, zip yourself up," she said, gesturing to Harold.

Sister Doomus extracted the key from her pocket, and she watched Shelly help Harold pull his shitty diaper back up. While he held it in place, Shelly continued to assist him, lifting his pants over it. Once Harold was as decent as could be expected, she went for the keyhole.

When the door unlocked, the dark silhouette of an older balding man—about the same stature as Sister Doomus—was erected in the doorway. The shadowy figure took a step forward, finding the light.

"Father Davenport, welcome," she said.

"My, my, what a splendid group," he replied with a smile. When he grinned, his mouth brandished two abnormally sharp lower lateral incisors. He almost looked snake-like in appearance due to his God-given peculiar pokey teeth and strange flaking and leathery skin texture.

The dapper-aged priest wreaked of Old Spice and a peppermint candy that clicked against his teeth as he swirled it around his mouth. The purple and gold satin clergy stole hung draped around his collar and bore a pair of gilded crosses embroidered on each side of it.

When he stepped inside, Sister Doomus quickly closed and locked the door behind him. Despite his confident and cheerful stride, the children still seemed incredibly nervous. They watched him carefully as he headed to the boys' room on the other side of the class.

Father Davenport cracked the door open then looked back at Sister Doomus. "Send in whomever you believe requires confession today, Sister Doomus. I'll be waiting…" he whispered with a nefarious leer.

Sister Doomus couldn't help but grin to herself as she looked at the sad lot that she was supposed to teach. She licked her lips and said, "Shelly Trout…" She paused extra for the most agonizing and dramatic effect, "*And* Harold Harlow, please see Father Davenport in the confessional stall. Tell him of the sins you've committed, and may God have mercy on your souls."

FRESH STAINS

The rain was coming down heavily when I pulled up to The Lonely Bug. There were two police cars at the far end of the motel strip, and a slather of crime scene tape plastered across the door of Room 13. Felix's lumpy frame stood outside the room's entrance as he chatted hectically with the authorities. The motel looked vacant at the moment, which was highly unusual. I suppose our crooked clientele didn't exactly have a deep desire to be around men in uniform.

I pulled over in front of the office as I usually did. I decided not to approach Felix and the police. He'd noticed my arrival, and I knew he would let me know when or if I could begin cleaning.

He continued his exchange for a few more moments and then nodded at the officer he was speaking with. He fixed his gaze in my direction and began moving toward me.

I unbuckled my seatbelt and hopped out of the car. Then I jogged with haste, trying to avoid the sprinkler-worthy rainfall that had just started, and entered the office.

Felix looked like he'd been standing in the rain for an hour, his thinning hair was positioned manically above the fat purple bags under his eyes. He looked like he'd been without rest—the typical horndog hounding that comprised the fibers of his DNA seemed absent, which I was grateful for. The stress was clearly having its way with him.

"What's going on?" I asked.

"Christ, you don't wanna know, but I suppose you're gonna need to anyway," he explained, making his way to the rear room behind the office.

"Follow me," Felix said, collapsing onto the scratchy toffee-toned couch that sat in the back room.

I stepped just inside the dingy doorway and asked, "Is someone hurt or something?"

"Yeah, you could say that, the big hurt, unfortunately for them. Some fuckin' pimp and his working girl. I'm not gonna lie, it was really bad. He musta pissed someone off real good. It looked like Jack the Ripper spent the night in that fuckin' room," he muttered.

"Jesus."

"Amen."

"Do… do they know why?" The concept of that breed of violence injecting itself back into my life was terrifying. We have a lot of scum that venture into our cheap rooms, and occasionally an argument or two, but nothing like this has ever happened before.

"Cops think it's drug-related, like most of the other shit that goes on around here. Anyhow, they've been here all night. Pig outside says they are just about finished with the crime scene. They've got the bodies cleared out, but there's a hell of a mess in there, Vera. I'm gonna need you to make that your top priority. The longer we wait, the harder it's gonna be to get all that blood up."

"You want *me* to clean it?"

"That's your fuckin' job, isn't it? Don't worry, I got something that will make it way easier. I had to with the way those fuckin' savages left it."

An eerie feeling began unfolding inside my belly like skeletons were dancing on my grave. A dark intuition smacked me across the face, it begged me not to ask.

"What did you get?"

"It's in the closet, check it out," he said, gesturing to the door inside the back room. "About an hour ago, I hit up Santino's Flea Market, right down the road there. Now it's an older model, but supposedly, it's one of the better ones, and the price was right."

As the door creaked open, I couldn't believe my eyes. Dread drenched my loins, nausea nibbled at my stomach, and hell bore its way back into my brain.

There it sat, the Bissell SC (self-contained) 1632 model. With the same white oval frame, slate base, and pink stripe around the container. The transparent base that normally held the water was empty, but the flashes in my mind impregnated the space with anguish-inducing abhorrence.

The blood that injected rapidly was fresh again. The wads of newly butchered humanity floated. The gory clumps of hair gathered at the base. The undeveloped and pulverized parts of the child I never had lingered. The child that was stolen from me, and replaced with Harold...

The singular inanimate object that was the tipping point for my entire downfall once again stood proudly before me. The device that was used like a weapon against my womb to pull the remnants of my dead child from my body, was a memory that I had tried to erase and lock away. Via a cruel coincidence, it had returned, and there was no escaping it.

I became dizzy and fell backwards as a murder-worthy scream left my lungs. But my disturbing wail was quickly stunted by the hot vomit that flew up from my hatch. Everything in front of me got fuzzy. I could hear Felix rambling in the background, but that faded away moments later, along with my vision.

I wasn't sure how long it took me to regain my bearings, but it felt like just a few minutes later, Felix was looming over me, tapping me on the cheek.

"Vera, what the hell happened? Are you okay?" he asked.

I paused for a moment and reregistered what had just transpired. My eyes found the Bissell in the closet again—it was real, it wasn't a dream.

"I-I can't clean that room," I explained to Felix.

Felix rose from the crouched position of concern and revisited his towering, domineering stance. All the care that was there previously vanished from his eyeballs.

Felix gritted his teeth before finally loosening them to speak. "I'm only gonna say this once. You don't clean that room, you don't have a fuckin' job."

***

After the police cleared out, I reluctantly pulled the Bissell up to the entrance of Room 13. It was the last thing I ever thought I'd be doing, but I had little choice in the matter. Felix was scum, I knew he had no qualms about sending me packing. I needed the money… *we* needed the money.

As the anxiety pulsated in my chest, I inserted the key and unlocked the door. The sticky tape ripped open and my eyes were treated to a horror that I hadn't seen the likes of in years…

At first, I thought it was probably a stabbing due to the sheer amount of blood that saturated the carpets and bedding. But when I noticed the little bits of flesh and fragments of skull that decorated the pools, it made me think that someone must have been bludgeoned to death. Maybe it was both?

"Excuse me, miss?"

The voice behind was unexpected, and in conjunction with the gory details of the murder scene, I couldn't help but let out a yelp of fright.

When I turned around, there was a girl standing in the downpour wearing a leather skirt that was too short for church. She couldn't have been far removed from her graduation day, although she didn't seem like the type that necessarily attained a diploma. Her licorice lipstick, wild hair, and midnight fingernails made her seem quite gloomy. She gave off an aura of uncertainty. The stench of darkness oozed out of her clogged pores, emitting immoral pheromones. But the look in her eyes and tone of her speech told a different story—something tender and naïve.

But when her wide childish pupils rested on my mashed, malformed face, which was intertwined with my own hectic expression of mania, I returned the favor. She seemed just as afraid of me as I was of her. I'm sure the butcher shop backdrop didn't help her feel any more at ease, but she quickly found her words.

"I-I'm sorry to bother you, miss. I just… I really need to ask you something," she said.

"Who are you?" It was the only question that seemed reasonable at the moment.

"I'm Tina. I'm friends with the people that were staying in this room. Maybe friends is the wrong word… but I was staying in here too," she explained.

A shudder traveled down her spine. I could tell she was telling the truth. I could tell she had peeked at the bloody mess, still trying to understand how lucky she was that she hadn't become an extension of it. I nodded my head, not really sure what to say or where it was going.

"The people in here… they left something… something that was owed to me," she explained.

The water welling in her miserable eyes was better than any lie detector test. When you've lived through extreme trauma, like I have, you just know. And my diagnosis was, whatever the last inhabitants of Room 13 had taken from her wasn't nearly worth what she was trying to recoup. She did a great job acting like she wasn't damaged, but we were two peas in a pod.

"I'd like to get it… if that's okay with you?" Her shyness made me like her even more; something that doesn't typically happen when I encounter a stranger.

"Well, I'm Vera, Vera Harlow," I said, offering my hand.

She stepped into the room and out of the elements, accepting the gesture. Her slender fingers wrapped gently around my own, and she said, "You already know I'm Tina, but my last name's Sparks."

Tina wasn't expecting it and neither was I, but from the handshake, I pulled her in closer and wrapped my other arm around her. I gave her a loose hug and whispered into her ear, "It'll be okay, you'll find a way to get past it."

I could hear the emotion manifest in her sinus. She held in the tears and sobs like she'd been practicing an entire lifetime. But I heard the very beginning of the pain, then, like a car trying to start but not turning over, she was able to bottle it. We had much in common.

"Thank you," she whispered. "How did you know?"

I softly pulled away from her and recalibrated my gaze to her eyes, "Have you looked at my face?" I asked, offering a cheesy grin.

She couldn't help but laugh. A little shiny snot bubble expanded from her nose and she quickly used her sleeve to wipe it away, along with a few tear streaks that had escaped.

"What are you doing hanging around this place? It's usually not this bad," I said, gesturing to the human remains. "But, let's just say I don't think the next president is coming out of here," I joked, closing and locking the door. If Felix woke up from his nap, I didn't want him seeing us.

"Ha, you're really funny. I feel like… like you should be a comedian or something, not a cleaning lady."

"I used to be a whole lot funnier… I guess sometimes it just takes meeting the right person to bring it out of me. But seriously, what are you doing here?"

"I just…" it was clearly hard for her to say it. "I just don't have anyone, Vera. I'm alone." She drew her shoulder-length wet hair out of her line of vision. "Entirely and indefinitely alone."

"I'm sorry. What happened to your parents, if you don't mind me asking?"

"A car wreck took 'em just before I hit middle school.

After that, it was off to Uncle Paul's house. He was the one that took care of me. He took care of me real fuckin' good."

There was an awkward gap of silence, but I didn't want to interject. I wanted her to continue. I wanted her to get it out. It was obviously eating her alive.

"I finally found the courage to leave, just got tired of him fuckin' me. I made a decision. I knew that my life was gonna be hell no matter what road I went down. It may as well be my flavor of choice. I figured, this way, I'd choose when it happens and make some money at least. Boy, was I wrong. The two sick fucks that were in this room... they turned me out. I thought it was bad with Uncle Paul, but that looks like fuckin' Disneyland compared to what they did to me."

I could see the weight lifting off of her. I could see the screaming shadows of the demons tearing away from her being. It didn't solve the past, but it was a subtle natural therapy. It would help her somehow, that much I knew.

"I'm terribly sorry, Tina. That must have been hard to say, but I'm really glad you did. I lost my folks too. Much later in life and due to natural causes, but it wasn't easy. And like you, I was tortured relentlessly. I had my baby taken. I had my sexuality and identity taken. I had my entire LIFE taken from me. I wasn't born with this face, it was scrambled and shamed by society. Believe me, I stand beside you, looking at the gates of hell, wondering what day I'm gonna get the guts to put a gun in my mouth and just finish this sick joke of a routine... but I still have hope. It's not a lot of hope, nowhere near enough to place a bet on, but I still have it. And you should, too."

The intensity of the conversation felt soul-shaking. I hadn't woken up intending to get this emotional or spiritual, but in a bizarre way, it felt good. My mind felt like it had suddenly been jolted back to life. I remembered my struggle today, and it wasn't pretty. But I had not scratched and clawed my way back to routine like a tiger working its way up the side of a mountain for nothing. I hadn't come this far to let it all swirl its way down the toilet bowl.

Tina was once again holding back tears. Clearly, she'd been moved by my words, but I had one more thing to say. "So, I hope that whatever they owed you doesn't control you. I hope that it's worth enough for you to pick a new destiny. Because I would really fuckin' love to know that at least one of us is going to make it."

We both broke down in tears and found each other's embrace again. We let it all out for a few more minutes before finally gathering the reserve to compose ourselves.

"Alright, well, the police probably bagged up most of what was in here as evidence, but you're welcome to have a look. I've got to start cleaning…"

"He makes *you* clean this up? That's fucking horrible."

"Eh, it wouldn't be the first time," I said with a smile.

I ventured into the bathroom, bringing the Bissell along with me. As I started to fill up the vacuum with water, I watched Tina set the room's lone chair up against the wall. She stood on top of it and then removed a screwdriver from her black purse. The carry bag had a maroon broken heart that looked slick and drippy stitched into the center of it. It almost seemed a little too appropriate for Tina considering her sad situation.

She quickly unscrewed three of the four screws holding a vent face on the top of the wall.

"Even the best cops can't find everything. And I'm betting…" Tina explained, putting the final twist on the last screw. "I'm betting that they didn't find it."

She set the face of the vent down on top of the tube and reached her hand inside and upward. When it returned, her palm was occupied by a bulky clear bag with a substantial amount of transparent, glass-like material inside.

"What is that?" I asked the question but felt like I knew the answer. I'd seen plenty of it around the motel in the past.

"Crystal meth."

"Oh… what are you going to do with that?"

"Don't look at me like that, I'm not gonna do it, okay? I'm gonna sell it. Once I sell it, like you said, I'm moving on and *never* fucking looking back."

I nodded my head and thought about what she'd said as I added some squeezable soap into the heart of the Bissell. She'd just finished screwing the vent back in and put the flathead in her purse when she engaged me again. The look in her eyes was like a daughter that had let her mother down.

"It's the only way. Without this, I don't have a chance. One quick deal, and I can finally move on."

"I really hope so—"

A thunderous rapping at the front door suddenly struck hard. I sure as shit wasn't expecting anyone…

"Who the fuck is that?" Tina whispered.

My heart started racing, my mind started calculating. I was looking around for a solution. My eyes found the tiny bathroom window that sat behind me.

"Come here, quick!" I whispered excitedly. I slid the window sideways and said, "You need to leave, now."

I helped Tina up into the opening, she balanced herself for another moment and looked into my eyes. "Vera, thank you," she said before pushing her way through the window and dropping to the ground below.

The pounding only grew louder on the door, and now a stern male voice from behind it said, "Police, open up!"

When I unlocked the door and opened it, there was a tall clean-cut man in a soaked trench coat and brown hat that forced his way inside immediately. He was less taken aback by the disfigurement than most people initially greeting me.

"I'm sorry, I thought it was safe to start cleaning, sir," I said as humbly as I could.

"It is…" the man said, adding a shade of suspicion to his persona. "Felix said you'd be in here… but why'd you lock the door?"

"Not sure if you heard the news, but two people got savagely murdered in here last night. Would *you* feel comfortable cleaning in here alone with an unlocked door?"

The man squinted his eyes at me, further sizing me up, "Alright, I suppose you're right," he replied.

"Why are you here? Mister…"

"I'm here because, a lot of times, killers will return to the scene of their crime afterward. It's more common than you think. Sometimes they've left something behind. Which is exactly why I'm here."

He began to peruse the room, looking, inspecting, and intimately scrutinizing his surroundings. "The name's Wells, Detective Wells. I'm just doing a little check-up, Vera. It is Vera, correct? Vera Harlow?"

I nodded my head.

"Police on scene cleared out a couple of hours ago. So, now would really be the ideal time for the culprit to return and tie up any loose ends. In some cases, they'll watch the crime scene be processed from afar, just patiently waiting to find an opportunity back inside."

"Cops also can just flat-out miss things. It's a high-stress job, a lot of shit can go on and a lot of shit can go wrong. So, I like to take a second look. Especially when a crime's as violent and cold-blooded as this one is. Yup, this one's a doozy. It's definitely one of the worst scenes I've been around in some time."

Detective Wells scratched at the stubble on his chin and then turned back towards me. I could tell he was cooking up a question in that egotistical skull of his.

"But you don't seem too bothered by it. Looks like it's just another normal day for you. Why is that?"

"You should be able to take one look at me and know that answer, Detective. Is it really detective? Must've been recently promoted, I guess," I replied without hesitation. I'd bury him in his own game of mental chess if he wanted to play it that way. I didn't have a damn thing to lose and wasn't in the mood for his swinging-dick antics.

His expression dove deeper into the recklessness he'd been trying to overshadow in his demeanor.

"Wow, you got a mouth on you," Detective Wells replied, laughing to himself. "Listen, I'm not here to bust your balls, I just want you to look me in the eye and answer one question. Did anyone come back in this room?"

"No."

"Okay," he replied, extracting a card from the inside of his trench coat. He set his card on the desk and tapped his finger's twice on top of it.

"Well, if anybody does, make sure that you call me, understood?"

I nodded my head again and watched him disappear out into the relentless rain. As soon as he left, I shut the door and let out a big huff of relief. It had been a while since I felt adrenaline like that. It was good to know I still didn't rattle under pressure.

I wasn't sure if what I did was the right thing, but it felt like the right thing to me. I would have a few hours to think about it while I cleaned. The whole ordeal had done a good job of distracting me from reliving my own horror. From thinking about when The Slob stuck this vacuum inside of me. From thinking about where I was in life as a result of it.

But as I turned on the Bissell and ran the head down the rug, it felt right. I could run away from it and try to forget who I was, or I could embrace it and use it to my advantage like I'd just done to 'Detective' Frank Drebin moments ago.

As the blood swirled into the clear sudsy water at the base of the Bissell, I couldn't help but view it as a metaphor for my own existence. What was once so clean and pure had been contaminated with filth and violence. I was, and always would be, one big swirling cyclone of hell, horror, and hope.

THE STRAW THAT BROKE THE SOLDIER'S BACK

Daniel sat dejectedly in his wheelchair by his bedside. The collection of empty bourbon bottles littered the floor, and dozens more were piled up in the corner of his room. There wasn't much space available for him to move around, but he didn't plan on moving much.

The television was shut off for once. It was a dangerous place to be for a man at Daniel's juncture—alone with one's thoughts. He lifted up the bottle of Evan Williams to his lips and took down multiple mouthfuls.

During the day, the only thing he had was time to think. Unexpectedly, the nerdy voice of Dr. Plankton had made its way between his ears: "You're still a family, aren't you?"

That was a hell of a question. While his initial answer was undoubtedly no, he had begun to wonder more about it. He'd begun to think about what the word family meant to him. The dictionary sitting cracked open atop his dirty sheets offered two definitions.

The first indicated that a family was, 'all the descendants of a common ancestor.' That definition made him angry. That version felt like his heart was being prodded with a steel spike. It reminded him only of everything that had been taken from him.

The second definition was far more thought-provoking. It read, 'a group of one or more parents and their children living together as a unit.' This seemed to be what old Dr. Plankton was referring to back inside his office.

Seeing family through that lens was a lot closer to what they had under their roof. And while the sour taste of his tortures tied into the first definition was still resonating in his mouth, maybe there was something being overlooked. Maybe he was too focused on everything that had been ripped away from him, instead of what he'd been given.

Part of Daniel wondered if it was him. If it was his own insecurities with fathering the child of a man who he'd like to nail to a cross. In his mind, Harold was horrible, but in the seven years they'd lived under the same roof, he hadn't really tried either.

He didn't want to let go of his hate for the human scum that was Harold's father, and every time he looked at him, it was merely a reminder. Maybe that was the problem and part of why the boy wasn't developing. Maybe he needed a real father figure that actually cared. What if he could find a way to let go? Would it change anything?

In the very beginning, he tried. Despite his resentment of Vera and her decision to keep Harold, he put on his game face and smiled for the pictures. But as Harold's grotesque features developed, they mirrored his father more. And his bizarre behavior grew alongside them. It reminded Daniel of the stories that Vera had told him. It enraged him.

SON OF THE SLOB

But with Dr. Plankton's hopeful words swirling around in his head, and a pool of bourbon swirling around in his guts, the idea somehow seemed plausible. Maybe he had just needed someone outside of his immediate family to suggest it to him. Butterflies scurried about his abdomen as he made the decision—he was going to try.

Daniel gently set the bottle down at his bedside and maneuvered his wheelchair in the tight space. Once he'd finally gotten it around, he opened the door to his room and wheeled himself into the hallway. The space was tight, but Daniel was able to trudge through the debris, and even shifted a few of the bags out of the way. He hadn't felt so motivated since he could remember.

The wheels came to a halt in front of Harold's door, but before he considered going in, he looked down the hall. There was no sign of Vera, no lights on or anything. He was a bit drunk, but not so much that he couldn't tell by that point in the evening Vera should have been home already.

"Where the fuck is she?" he whispered to himself.

WHACK! The unexpected noise nearly made his ears pop. *WHACK!* It sounded off again, just as loud as the first time. *WHACK!* It was obvious exactly where the unsettling noise was coming from. Each time he heard it, the door right in front of him shook.

A shuddersome somberness took hold of him; he was aware that what he was about to see probably wasn't going to correlate to the feelings that he was looking to express to his strange stepson. The dread took hold of him as his hand took hold of the dirty doorknob and slowly began to turn it.

The scene painted before him shouldn't have been a surprise; he'd seen the likes of it before, just in different manifestations. It was the epitome of the reason why Daniel felt the way he did before he decided to act on his spontaneous change of heart.

Harold held his math book above his head and made eye contact with Daniel. He didn't speak a word to him, he just watched the hardcover come down in the blink of an eye.

WHACK!

When the book hit the ground this time, the mammoth mother rat twitching beneath it came undone. As black fur caved inward, and the vermin's body crunched, the excess of blood contained in the rodent's morbidly obese frame erupted upward. The blow was placed randomly, but strictly followed Murphy's Law to a tee—what can go wrong will go wrong.

The low probability of it drenching Daniel's face as he sat slack-jawed didn't matter. This was a 'family' that found a way to achieve the most morbid unbelievabilities with regularity. This was a 'family' that was a magnet for the grotesque. And as Daniel collected the hot and undoubtedly diseased blood and spat it out from his palate, he had his epiphany—this was a 'family' no more.

Harold set the gut-smeared textbook beside him and stuck both of his hands into the cavernous gash, pulling it apart in opposite directions. Once it was separated, he picked up a handful of the slimy organs inside and slipped it into his agape jowl.

Daniel sat speechless and wiped the blood off his face as best he could, while Harold serenaded him with the slobbery sounds of the slick organs mashing and compressing. The vermin juices escaped Harold's orifice and dribbled down his stubby chin as he took hold of the hairy half that the rat's head was attached to.

While the cranium had been collapsed, it was still tough. The whiskery exterior of the foul thing tickled his tongue upon entry. It caused Harold to emit a childish giggle before crushing down and shifting his demeanor to a more primal version.

Daniel curled his lips and put his face in his bloody hands as the slurping and crunchy sounds echoed in his skull. "NO! NO! NO! NO!" he screamed.

His loud wails didn't provide the slightest hesitation, or prevent Harold from gnawing through the neck and spine of the gnawer and ripping it from the upper body entirely.

Daniel turned his wheelchair back out of the room and slammed the door shut as quickly as possible. His hands slipped off the wheels initially because they were saturated in the rat blood. He wiped them on his pants and sped back to his room.

Once inside, he immediately cracked open a new bottle of Evan Williams and washed down the neck of it. He placed the bottle between his legs and headed to the dresser next. In the far corner was a picture taken of Daniel in Vietnam. On his side was a black man with an afro that looked to be about the same age as Daniel. They both had smiles on their faces, but the joy was a farce.

He smashed the frame and ripped the photo out like his life depended on it. He took another generous gulp before making his way back to the telephone. Daniel lifted up the receiver and then flipped over the picture. On the back, still legible, there was a phone number written in blue ink. Daniel keyed in the number at lightning speed.

The phone rang four times before he heard a click, "Yeah?" the voice on the other said.

"Morris?" Daniel asked.

"Who the fuck wants to know?"

"It's Danny."

"Danny? Danny who?"

"Danny Harlow, from Nam."

"Danny Harlow? Is this a joke? You gotta be shittin' me, man! I figured you was dead, brother!"

"Not yet, but sometimes it feels that way. Listen, I'm not gonna bullshit you, Morris. I'm in a real bad spot… I got…" Daniel started to break down but tried to hold it together. "I got no one else to call, man. Would you… would you come and pick me up? I need a place to stay for a while and get my head on straight."

Morris paused for a moment as if contemplating the request. He hadn't heard a peep from Daniel in decades, but he'd been around long enough to understand a call out of the blue was usually never good news.

Morris recalled a few of their many interactions together overseas. The one-in-a-million odds that two people living so close to each other would get drafted into the same platoon was something he could never forget. Back in the times of gruesome violence and anxiety, they grew to be brothers. Recalling the dope band venues, events at the civic center, and things that happened back before they were killing strangers helped them both pass the time and keep their sanity within arm's length.

The Burger Billy's restaurant was one place that they talked about incessantly. Two juicy patties, brioche buns, and Billy's secret sauce. During wartimes, they would've given anything to get a combo deal together. They both thought it was the best burgers in the state. They swore they'd meet up to celebrate once the war was over, but after Daniel got maimed, how could they celebrate?

Morris called a few times, but after no follow-up, he got the picture. He figured the man was probably suicidal. Morris hadn't been paralyzed himself, yet still, he found himself thinking about ending things on more than one occasion.

"Look, I-I understand if you can't—"

Morris cut off Daniel, "Hey, Danny boy, what was that shit we used to say every time we went out into the jungle and thought we was gonna die? Do you remember?"

The tears were pouring like the rain outside, Daniel could barely manage the words, "Brothers till the end."

"That's right, man. Brothers till the end."

DON'T GO IN THE BASEMENT

By the time I finished with Room 13, the hands of the clock had pushed hours past the end of my shift. Not that Daniel was normally on the lookout for me or anything, so I guess it didn't matter, but it was kind of sad in a way that I wasn't really sure if he'd even notice. That was the nature of our relationship these days.

While the amount of time required to get the room in rentable shape bordered on miraculous, it didn't really feel that way. It flew by, probably because I was more focused on the carousel of thoughts parading through my mind than the actual task at hand.

The numerous fractures in my foundation that served as the crux of my destruction and downfall. The overwhelming mess at the house. The rotting dichotomy that Daniel and I shared. My mutant of a son. Would he ever be normal?

While all of those things and more were on my mind, I unexpectedly found myself spending the most time thinking about Tina. I really do like that girl. It's not every day that you have an opportunity to connect, and I mean truly connect, with a person who has been through what you have. I really do wish the best for her; she deserves a chance, at least from what I could tell.

The room was about as clean as it was going to get. It was night and day from when I first walked inside. You couldn't even really tell that anything had happened, but you could still feel that something did. I could anyway.

Sometimes, after a horrible event occurs in a place, a weight continues to hang inside it. The darkness attaches itself like a parasite, and the event and location aren't just synonymous anymore, they're one. I was quite familiar with the concept seeing that I'd been trying to stop that very same macabre metamorphosis from happening to my house, ever since Harold had taken his first breath.

While my last interaction with Daniel wasn't what I'd aspired for it to be, it seemed like it might be easier to talk now. The silence had been broken, leaving the opportunity to communicate feeling more inviting than it had in months.

While the thought of him striking Harold still grinded my gears, the more I pondered the situation, the more I realized that I was wrong, too. I reprimanded him with the same cruelty that he'd dished out. For that much, I owed him an apology. Maybe if I made peace and asked him for forgiveness, he would, in turn, see the error in his own actions and follow suit.

After I finished throwing away the DNA-drenched trash in the dumpster, I entered the office and put the cleaning supplies away. I was happy to see that Felix had left for the evening, and Frank, who worked the front desk overnight, had taken his place. I liked Frank mostly because we never felt the need to interact much. Typically, our shifts didn't overlap, but when they did, there was no hostility. Just a simple nod of the head and reasonably measured respect.

SON OF THE SLOB

If there was any night that it would have made sense to have a conversation spark between us, it was tonight. But I think Frank could tell that I'd been through the wringer. He knew what I was doing in that room. But instead of initiating pointless gossip when I was already dead tired, he just whispered, "Have a good night, Vera," and nodded his head like he always did.

"You too," I replied, grateful that he saw beyond his own late-night entertainment and curiosity.

On the drive home, the raindrops only got heavier, pinging over and over on the tinny exterior of the wagon's roof. I kept trying to think of what to say to Daniel, but the radio droning on in the background was a distraction.

"The rental truck that was parked outside of the Alfred P. Murrah Federal Building is still believed to be the location of the bomb. The body count is up to one-hundred-and-thirty-seven as of this evening, but the blast in Oklahoma City injured hundreds in addition. In other news, the Chicago area is still buzzing about the return of Michael Jordan. After announcing that his experimental venture into minor league baseball with the Birmingham Barons has finally concluded. His—"

I turned the radio off, wondering how someone could want to kill so many people for seemingly no reason. I suppose the reason didn't really matter—whatever it was, the motive wouldn't be able to justify the horror. The attack had been all over the television for weeks, and on the front of every newspaper in the country. Most were well informed on the topic, but I had little time to learn much about it or pay attention. I was busy cleaning up the relentless disasters in my own life.

I sat in silence the rest of the drive, trying to anticipate what I would be walking into at home. There were many dark projections always lingering in my brain that seemed like they were just waiting to manifest. Some of them had even come to life over the years, but thankfully, the more gruesome renditions had stayed in the fantasy realm.

Before I could figure out what potential scene to dread, I was stepping through the threshold of the doorway. The scurrying of the vermin rang through my ear canals as usual, but I wasn't going to think about it; Daniel was still heavy on my mind.

I followed the hallway, navigating the trash heaps of clutter, bypassing Harold's room, which was a break in my typical routine. As I approached Daniel's door, the anxiety sunk its fangs into my belly.

"Here goes nothing…" I whispered.

I pushed my fear aside and knocked gently on the door three times. There was no answer or sound in response. In fact, the normal sounds of the television that usually serenaded me through the fractured hunk of wood were absent too. It was later than normal, but not bedtime…

"Daniel?" I called out. After a few more seconds, I was officially concerned.

"Daniel, is everything alright?" Such a stupid question in the grand scheme of things, but he knew the context I was phrasing it in.

"I'm coming in." My concern was highlighted in the tone I projected, but it would not be relieved by uncovering the scene, or lack thereof, on the other side of the door.

The chilly dark room was empty. Even before I could flip the light switch, I knew that much. Daniel was gone… where he'd left to, I could only wonder.

While the shock hit me in the face like a hard slap, the reality was, if he'd left, one thing was for sure. He hadn't taken Harold for the ride along with him. I couldn't imagine that he'd ventured to another area of the house but I needed to check quickly. I also needed to find Harold…

"Daniel?! Harold?!" I wailed, distress further increasing the volume of each word I spoke.

When I opened the door to Harold's room, his nightlight was on and his comforter was strewn about the floor surrounded by random toys and trash.

"Harold!" I yelled.

I examined the living room and found nothing, then I navigated to the kitchen. There was no sign of him in the pantry or my room either. I stepped out on the porch and opened the door to the backyard. My heart began pounding harder; my eyes had already adjusted to the darkness and I could see that neither of them were in the enclosed space.

There was only one place left to check—the basement.

"Did he fucking kill him?" I couldn't help but wonder.

I didn't particularly like going down there. It was creepy and cluttered. Harold knew he shouldn't ever go alone. I'd found him in the darkness of the cellar a few months back 'exploring himself.' I had to reprimand him, and explained that Daniel and I would punish him much worse next time if he ventured into the basement again by himself. He'd heeded that warning without issue up until now. But at the moment, I couldn't be sure if he'd gone back to his old ways, or if something even worse had transpired between Harold and Daniel.

I turned the light on and made my way. With each step I took down the filthy flight of stairs, the wood cried out with a lengthy groan. With each creaky step, my fear surged.

"Harold? Daniel?" I said, finally reaching the bottom.

There was no response as I rounded the corner. The light from the staircase trickled into the room and softly illuminated the disturbing scene before me. Amid the boxes and bags of junk, in the center of the basement floor sat Harold. He'd stripped down naked, and his tar-caked teeth nearly disappeared in the darkness. But to my trained pupil, I could clearly see he was smiling. His puffy sausage-like hands—one red hand and one brown—looked like they'd been pressed together in prayer…

Harold stood silently before me in all his obese glory. As I moved closer, I saw the smattering of excrement and the deep red that peppered his frame and oozed off a variety of areas. I didn't have to imagine what the liquids were; as alarming as his own corporal presentation was, the wicked waste and aftermath of his deeds beside him told the story.

The outline that stretched the length of a few feet was one that Harold undoubtedly familiarized himself with at school—a cross. But the blasphemous nature of the materials used to bring his bizarre blueprint to life were nothing short of nauseating.

The general outline of the warped religious symbol was comprised of his nostril stinging defecation. It was smeared across the dusty stone floor, creating a cross that was a few feet long and wide. The watery nature of his discharge made it appear as if he'd eaten something that had made him sick.

Additionally, it also seemed that Harold had been trying to deal with the rat problem in his own way. But instead of rat poison, snap or sticky traps, Harold was using pure bare-handed brutality.

The collection of rodent body parts, bones, and innards had been draped throughout the messy shit-smeared paths in an almost decorative manner. Some of the torn apart hunks of rat remains were squirming with their final death tremors. The violence had found me again.

The creation was hideous; like a mental wart multiplied and come to life. I felt the sickness kicking around in my guts, ready to surge up in mortifying fashion. As the lack of lunch and surplus of coffee I'd consumed at The Lonely Bug launched onto the floor beside me, somehow, I was able to remain dry-eyed.

I was still too wound up to be emotional. Thankfully, the fear was over for the most part... at least I knew where Harold was. His mess was an atrocity, but still, it was something that was easily fixable. His mind remained the problem.

Part of me believed that he was trying to do something good. He was translating the teachings that Sister Doomus had relayed to him in school, but somehow, that translation had gotten majorly fucked up.

He was trying. Trying to make something for God, trying to say a prayer. But what was he praying for? I could see not knowing the answer to that question starting to gnaw on me in the future.

I knew that the more I would dwell on it, the crazier it would drive me. I pushed it to the back of my mind and saved it for later. Besides, there was a much better question that still remained at hand—where the hell was Daniel?

WORSE THAN WAR

"Shit, Danny boy, that's about as bad, if not worse, than anything we seen overseas," Morris said, scooping the bottle of Jim Beam off of the coffee table.

Daniel's wheelchair was parked on the side of the couch next to Morris as two unhygienic glasses began to fill up with the harsh brown alcohol.

"You damn well deserve another drink after that shit," he continued, topping off the glass.

"It doesn't even feel real anymore, my life feels like some kind of delusion, some sick nightmare," Daniel explained, reaching out for the drink.

"I suppose I could say the same, I might've come back from Nam, but part of me is still there. Maybe even more fucked up is that part of there is still here," Morris said, pointing to the temple on the right side of his head.

"I thought I'd beat it for a while. When Vera was pregnant, everything was falling into place. I found a way to let the past go. But doing that twice just don't seem possible to me…" Daniel confided, taking down a massive gulp of the glass.

"Brother, another man done beat your unborn child to a pulp and sucked it out of your wife with a mutha fuckin' vacuum cleaner. If that ain't bad enough, he replaced it with his own seed. You got a right to think that." Morris finished his glass like he was drinking water and quickly poured another out.

"You know me, I never been one to bullshit ya, Danny boy, I don't see how you could fix something like that. There would have only been one fix, but that option is already by the wayside."

"I begged her to get an abortion…" The look in Daniel's eyes held a compounded totality of hurt that most people wouldn't witness in five lifetimes.

"I know you did. You did everything you could. But there's no doubt that Vera… did I say it right this time?"

"Yeah…" Daniel replied dejectedly.

"There's no doubt Vera is fucked up in the head from all that. She was trying to do right by you, but just like the rest of us, she can't see down the line. She probably thought that baby was gonna bring the two of you together."

"I made it damn well clear that wouldn't be the case—"

"I know you did, but you know women, they always think they know what's best for a man. It's a damn shame things shook out that way, sounds like she was a hell of a lady. Most any girls I ever known don't see a wounded veteran as husband material. She's a saint for that," Morris said with a slight chuckle.

Morris only paused slightly to take another swig before continuing, "I know my old lady sure as hell didn't."

"I meant to ask where Beth was… I'm sorry, man, I'm just so fucked up that it goes beyond basic courtesy. You always talked about her so glowingly," Daniel said.

"She was something else," Morris replied, staring at the wall enveloped by a moment of nostalgia.

"What happened?"

"Let's just say my transition back to civilian life wasn't so smooth."

"What do you mean? You heard the shit I been through, trust me, you ain't gonna shock me. Sometimes it feels good to get it out, at least for me it did, anyway…"

Morris pondered the offer and took another mouthful before continuing, "You ever get night terrors? Wake up in the middle of the night and, BOOM, you're back in the jungle again?"

Daniel realized it was a question, but more of a rhetorical nature. He just listened as Morris continued on.

"And you… you just can't turn it off. It's embedded in your fuckin' brain. You see Charlie everywhere. And you see what he done to your brothers everywhere. Sometimes it blurs your vision."

Daniel nodded his head slowly in agreement. Although the degree of post-traumatic stress disorder that plagued Morris never reached anything like that for him, he still wanted Morris to feel comforted by his support and not think he was alone.

"Danny, I've slept with a fuckin' gun under my pillow since '73. One night, not too far after we came back, I woke up. I would've sworn to God himself that Charlie was in my closet. I heard the rustle in the bushes behind the doors in the darkness. I smelled the stagnant swamp water that he was watchin' me from. I heard him whisper in that fuckin' gook gibberish. He wanted me dead."

Morris made his fingers into the shape of a handgun and raised them up in front of him. "So, I raised my gun up and shot that mutha fucka."

He took another sip and set the empty glass down, only to immediately pour another.

"You want another?" he asked Daniel.

"Please."

As Morris finished filling them up, only about a quarter of the bottle remained.

"Do you know what was behind the other side of that closet door?" Morris asked.

Daniel shook his head.

"My son's room. The bullet went through the wall and into the pillow just a couple of inches beside his head."

"Damn..." Daniel replied not knowing what else to say.

"Beth packed up all her shit the next day, she didn't even have too much really. Seemed like she had one foot out the door since I got back. But she packed up all her shit and all of Joseph's shit, and I haven't seen either of them ever since."

There was a long moment of silence while they drank. Daniel didn't really know what to say, but he knew he had to say something.

"I'm sorry, man."

"It's alright, I've grown to accept it. Don't really have a choice in the matter."

"Did you ever think of trying to reach out to them?"

Morris turned his head coldly toward Daniel. A snarl crept over his expression. "Now why the fuck would I wanna do that?"

"Times change, people change. That was a long time ago. I'm sure Joseph wants to know who his father is. I'm sure he thinks about it often, don't you?"

"Some things are better left in the dark. He was young enough that he hopefully don't have no memory of me at all. It's probably for the best. I'm sure he's doing just fine and don't need me comin' round and fuckin' his life up again," Morris mumbled.

Morris was starting to feel a little lightheaded from all the booze, but it wasn't anything that he couldn't handle. "It's the same with you and your boy, really."

"That ain't my fuckin' boy, Morris." Daniel's gear shifted faster and more drastically than a drag race between manual vehicles.

"Oh, you don't like it when the shoe is on the other foot I guess? Ain't that easy, is it?" Morris replied.

"That's not what I meant."

"Well, understand that it ain't all that different, except in my case, I'm the fucked up one. But I'm an adult and at least got the sense to stay clear and avoid making things worse. That boy at your house, whether you like it or not, he's depending on you. He didn't ask to be born."

Daniel wasn't convinced by the parallel he'd drawn, but he was glad to get an opinion from someone outside of the situation. It's hard to see the forest when you're a tree inside of it. It was food for thought that he might chew on at a later date once it sunk in.

At the same time, he felt guilty about it. Just up and leaving without saying a word was something that he never even considered doing until what he'd seen that evening. His psyche could only withstand so much until he had to make choices that ignored the interests of others.

He thought about calling her as he cradled the drink and brought it up to his lips again. It was probably the right thing to do, but he was too drunk for another argument. It would probably just be worse than the worry he'd left behind. While radio silence was imminent, it still didn't stop him from wondering how Vera was doing.

SIDEWAYS

Tina walked nervously down the road under the faint flicker of the streetlight. The fact that she had enough crystal in her purse to craft a fucking chandelier made her nervous. She was dressed like what she was—a hooker. The notion of being approached by a cop wasn't a far-fetched one.

She was thankful that the rain was starting to let up, but she had a lot of work to do still. She didn't want to hold onto the stash any longer than she had to. The imminent threat of a real danger, intertwined with her never-ending thoughts of paranoia, wasn't something she could deal with for more than a day.

Hopefully, it wouldn't be more than a few more minutes. She stepped into the smoke-filled barroom and immediately all eyes were on her. Not because any of the goons inside knew what she had—drugs or not, she was a good-looking young girl with a pussy that was half the age of the majority of the men eye-fucking her.

"Well, there you are, I was getting worried," Greg said.

A small measure of relief came over her upon seeing his grinning face. Greg Davis was an ex-boyfriend and petty criminal that she'd met while working. He accepted her for who she was, and treated her well enough. The problem was that he was a tweaker. Initially, he'd hidden it well, but the truth eventually became unavoidable.

He'd disappear for days on end for benders that were so wild they made James Brown look like the picture of health. Eventually, he always resurfaced, usually with a black eye or fat lip, and always with a thousand excuses. Greg still never lost his smile though, no matter how many teeth got knocked out of it.

His most pressing issue was that he'd do anything to score. There was no ask that was too absurd, no act that was too obscene. When he eventually stopped having sex with Tina, she started to catch on that something was wrong.

After discovering the gay scene downtown paid out some handsome party favors if you were willing to bend over, Greg's excess smashed through the roof. HIV was never something he'd thought about, but after he heard a rumor at the club that one of the men he'd done favors for was positive, he had no other choice but to get tested.

Tina respected Greg for telling her the truth. It couldn't have been easy. She got herself tested immediately and was relieved when the results came back negative. Greg could've been a scumbag and just kept fucking her, but he didn't. Their relationship wasn't exactly the contents of a romance novel anyway. Even after the fallout, they were able to stay friends, and more importantly, as far as that evening was concerned, occasional business acquaintances.

"Have a seat," Greg said, pulling out the stool beside him and brandishing a smile absent of a few pearly whites. "I was wondering if you were gonna show."

"I wouldn't have called you if I wasn't," she said, returning a much prettier grin. "Shit's just been crazy since Jermaine and Sierra got offed. That fuckin' room looked like a bloodbath. I never seen anything like it..."

"But you got it, right? You got the shit?"

"Yeah."

"Lemme see it," he whispered excitedly.

"Greg, relax, we're in a bar full of people. You can see it later. But you're not fuckin' doing a pinch until this deal is finished, you understand me?"

"Yeah, sure, okay," Greg rattled off in his jittery tone.

"If you do this right, you'll have more than you can handle. I'm gonna give you some money too. Hopefully, you'll just smarten up and get off the shit, use it to get out of this mess. But I'm not gonna be around to find out. After this, I'm fuckin' gone."

A melancholic glaze dripped over Greg's eyes. "I understand, Tina. I promise I won't fuck it up. You're a great girl… and I'm a fuck-up."

"You're not a fuck-up, Greg."

"It's okay, I know what I am. But I'm not too big of a fuck-up to realize that you deserve to be happy. I mean it, your life didn't go to shit because of anything you done. Me, on the other hand, maybe this is my punishment."

"Listen, you didn't exactly have it easy either. All I'm saying is, we have one deal to make, just one. If we can get through this together, then you'll have one more chance at redemption. Now, if you squander that, then you're officially a fuck-up," Tina giggled, tapping him on the nose, trying to find a way not to let her nerves eat her alive.

"You always got jokes," Greg said with a laugh.

"So, who's the buyer?"

"Some guy, Dino, I met downtown. I've known him for a few months."

"How do you know he's not connected?"

"Tina, the guy's just a fuckin' party monster! Connected people don't just bang blow in the bathroom of Vicki's with scum like me. He's chasing the dragon, not trying to bottle it," Greg explained.

"So, where does this Dino wanna meet us?"

"The docks."

"The docks? Why there?"

"Because he's got a boat."

"A boat? C'mon, Greg, don't bullshit me on this, the guy obviously has money if he has a boat."

"Tina, sweetheart, you're selling a fuckin' pound of crystal. I have news for you, whoever is buying that much is gonna need to have some scratch, you understand that, right? But if you don't wanna do it, just say the word. I can call the whole thing off. In fact, I can even stash the glass for you until we find another buyer—"

"Ha! Yeah, right. Just a fraction of this would kill most people, but somehow, I know you'd find a way to survive and get through it in a couple of weeks."

"Well?" Greg said with a smirk.

"I guess we'll just have to take a chance."

***

Dino was grinning ear to ear when Tina and Greg walked up to the massive boat. It was larger than either of them had anticipated it would be. He stroked his thin handlebar mustache with one hand and sipped on the ocean blue margarita resting in his other.

"I thought you guys weren't coming! You had me wondering pretty good," he asked, with a queer tinge to his voice. He waved the small silk scarf draped around his neck in their direction, beckoning the pair excitedly.

"Takes longer when you gotta walk, Dino," Greg smiled.

"Not a problem, I'm just excited. It's not every day a deal like this comes along…" he explained, waving them into the bowels of the massive boat.

Tina and Greg stepped inside the entrance and headed down a narrow hallway that had a red light at the end of it. Greg looked back for a moment as if to use his unsure expression to ask if they should continue to the end.

"Yup, it's all the way down. Nice and private, no one'll bother us on here," Dino said.

As they made their way around the corner, they were greeted by a luxurious leisure space. A place that street people like Tina and Greg had little chance of gracing outside of the situation at hand.

It was comprised of fancy benches with upholstered seating, expensive bottles of liquor, and dark ambient lighting. But it wasn't so much what the room was filled with that immediately struck a grave feeling of discomfort into Greg's gut... it was *who* it was filled with.

Dutch Jones sat in the center, smoking a blunt wrapped in forest green papers with a nasty scowl scraped into his expression. A full-grown iguana sat perched on his right shoulder, stoic and obedient. Behind the Terminator shades that hid his eyes laid a stare that was just as cold-blooded as the liquid running through his lizard's veins. That was also conveyed as he slowly stroked the platinum Colt pocket pistol with the gentle and sugary love a mother would have for her newborn.

He was flanked by a pair of hulking bald twins that could barely fit into their black t-shirt's. Corey and Cam Carter portrayed the definition of intimidation. Two men that the room was at the behest of upon their setting foot in it. They looked more like statues based on how their bodies had been carved out and the frightening state of blankness on their ingratiation-inducing faces.

Both Tina and Greg stopped dead in their tracks when they saw the terrifying trio. These were the type of men they were trying to avoid. They were the people that ended lives after arguments. They both knew they were fucked.

Greg was so intimidated and soul-shaken by Dutch's presence, he didn't even see Dino put the clear bag over his head. As the plastic sucked in and out, Greg's arms flailed wildly through the air. The Carter twins pounced on him and took over the assault.

Tina was briefly stunned by the sudden flash forward to violence. But by the time she got the idea that she needed to run, Dutch's pistol was already aimed at her skull.

"You need to have a seat, bitch, before I blow those dick-suckin' lips of yours all over the mini-bar," Dutch said.

Tina complied with the threat as Corey powered Greg to the shaggy rug. Cam lifted up his size fourteen and brought the heel down on the back of Greg's skull. The sickening crunch and subsequent bubbly gurgle and cry ripped Tina's heart out.

This was all because of her—Greg was going to die now because she wanted to try and cash out. The adrenaline shooting through her system made her shake in an orgasmic manner. Her hysteria and stress were audible as her lungs ballooned and shrunk in a cartoonish fashion.

"Keep that faggot's blood off my rug, you know he got the ninja," Dutch said coldly.

Despite Dino's lifestyle, he ignored the nasty comment. As far as he was concerned, Dutch could say whatever hateful shit was in his black heart as long as he was still getting his commission.

Cam weighed in one more neck-breaking boot before Greg's whimpers came to a halt. Greg was still breathing, but not thinking or moving as the clear plastic bag began to fill up with crimson like a thirsty tick's body.

"So, you found my ice. But instead of being a good Samaritan and returning back to me what you damn well know is rightfully mine, you tried to flip it. After Jermaine and the two-bit whore that burned me got tightened up, I'd have figured whoever came across it would've got the message. So, either you a fuckin' dummy, or you got a death wish. Which is it?"

Tina's chattering jaw tried to find words that could get her out of the scary situation. "I-I'm sorry," she said, pulling the fat taped-up brick of tweak out from her purse and setting it on the coffee table. "I had no idea it was yours, if I'd known, then—"

"Bitch, you know who the fuck I am. I'm the source. I'm the only mutha fucka slingin' shards round these parts, and that's because I exterminate the competition."

Dutch turned his head and looked into his lizard's eyes, "What you think, Philly? She know who I am?"

The crystal kingpin revisited his gaze back upon Tina's trembling frame. "And just like you know who I am, I know who your slutty ass is," he explained, once again raising the burner to her eye level. "And I know who this faggot, HIV-havin' ass is," he continued, moving the barrel toward Greg's motionless body that the Carter brothers still stood over dominantly. "Because I *am* the streets."

He set the gun down on his lap and let out a deep breath. "Now, I know you thought this was your come-up. I know what it's like to not have shit and finally get some shit. That's cool by me… unless it's *my* shit. If I let one person get over on me, well, I'm setting a dangerous precedent. So, as much as my heart bleeds for you, if I don't do nothing to you for eating off my plate, I'm inviting the next nigga to do the same. You understand?"

"I wouldn't say anything! I would… I would be gone, that's a promise," Tina explained, still rattled to the core.

"That ain't a solution. You might keep your mouth shut, but the streets is always watching… listening… talking. I'm afraid it's not that simple."

Dutch played with the ideas of how she should be handled in his mind for a few moments. A stew of his nasty pastimes swirled around inside his skull. Suddenly, a light bulb illuminated. He smiled and beckoned Dino over. He quickly obliged his request and leaned into Dutch while whispering something into his ear.

Dino nodded and approached the table in the back that had a variety of party favors and various drug paraphernalia strewn upon it. He took hold of the hypodermic needle and removed the cap from the end of it. The tip of the pointy steel glistened in the dim lighting.

"I'm feeling gracious today. You're not too far removed from being a child, and I understand, in youth, we make mistakes. I sure as fuck did. The best I can do is give you some time," Dutch explained.

Dino returned back to the Carter twins and whispered Dutch's message to them.

The pair of musclebound bastards closed in on her quickly. One kept her arms and body in check, and the second clasped his massive mitts on each side of her head.

Tina started to scream and jerk back and forth, the uncertainty of the situation helped her achieve a new tier of inner turmoil.

"Please, I'll do anything! Just don't hurt me—"

Tina's pleas were stunted by the handkerchief that Cam shoved into her mouth. He then wrapped his digits over her food hole and pressed her head back against the seating.

She watched in wide-eyed horror as Dino plunged the needle into Greg's static arm and carefully sucked out a full syringe tube of contaminated blood.

"I can give you some time, but it'll be a lot less time than you started off with. But you may need to find a new profession once the streets find out about this," Dutch explained.

Dino closed in with the shiny needle tip angled at her exposed eyeball. Cam kept her in a chin lock with his hand still over her mouth and used the other one to keep her eyelids spread.

As the steel pierced through the white of her eye, Tina did her best to keep still despite shaking uncontrollably. Dino pushed a quarter of the deadly blood into her orb before retracting the spike and moving down to her shaking wiry arm.

A fiend himself, Dino had found the stringiest veins for 'friends' in the most blown-up of arms. Poking a tube in a straight girl like Tina was an amateur task for a fella with such a degenerate background.

Once it slipped inside, the remainder of the blood was pushed out of the needle seconds later. Tina felt the diseased warmth intermingling with her own warmth. She was still alive but instantly felt like, for all intents and purposes, her life was over.

While the ghastly ordeal was transpiring, Dutch had broken off a buff bag of glass from the brick. He let it sit in the palm of his hand as his soldiers finished up.

Dino stepped away and set the dirty needle down on top of Greg's body. He let out a slight moan just as the twins joined him. Cam lifted up his black work boot and came down on the area of his cranium that was already cracked open. The weight and power sent a segment of his brains shooting upward through the gape like an overfilled pimple volcanically erupting.

He immediately stopped making noises and breathing. The clear bag on his head looked like a cannibal had just puked inside of it. Greg would never have to worry about his next fix ever again.

Tina, on the other hand, pressed her fingers gingerly against her irritated and inflamed eyeball, while Dutch watched her cry. Dutch was no dummy, he'd thought of a way to kill her, send a message to the streets, and still profit off her for the foreseeable future.

"Now, I know you a straight girl, but you gonna need this movin' forward," he explained, tossing a healthy bag of crushed glass at her.

Tina looked at the portion of foul chemicals sitting on her lap and tried to compose herself.

"I said fuckin' take it!" Dutch yelled.

She picked up the heavy bag of poison and slipped it back into her purse in an effort to avoid any further punishment being dished out.

"Now, you have fun with that," he grinned. "And if you need more, you know who to come to."

Dutch then turned his attention back to the Carter twins and sent them a slow nod. They turned around and grabbed Dino; Corey muscled his armpit over his throat and Cam stepped on his feet, holding him in place. The behemoth bent him backwards until his throat arched in a manner that caused a disturbing cracking noise to spring from his neck and spinal column and echo through the room.

Dutch gingerly brushed the side of his iguana's face as he watched Dino's lifeless body join Greg's on the floor.

"I hate fuckin' snitches," he mumbled.

ROOM 13

When I arrived back at The Lonely Bug the next morning, I parked the wagon some distance away from the front office. I kept my distance since Harold was in the backseat. I had no choice but to bring him—it was Saturday and I wasn't going to leave him to his own devices alone in the house.

After cleaning the blood and feces off of Harold last night, I felt dead tired and decided I would deal with his mess in the basement at a later time. I say that, but judging by the rest of the house, that's a gamble at best.

The only plan I could whip up under such short notice was to bring him with me. If I left him in Room 13, I could then work my way from Room 1 forward. Felix would only rent the rooms I cleaned, so it seemed like the most feasible plan to avoid detection.

I certainly wasn't going to explain my situation to him, it would only lead to more disgusting harassment and he probably wouldn't allow Harold to stay in the room without docking my pay. Felix was precisely that kind of asshole.

When I arrived inside, I opened the door carefully, not allowing the attached bells to jingle. Felix was in the back slumped over on the grimy couch while Jenny Jones rambled on about secret admirers in the background.

I quietly opened the closet and wheeled out my cleaning cart. Then I scooped up the keyring that allowed me access to all the rooms. Upon exit, the bells jingled and I jerked my head back in fear, but thankfully, Felix remained mid-snore.

I quickly pushed the cart up to Room 1, internally thanking Felix for his no-bullshit early checkout policies. He had no problem clearing out the scum every morning and they had finally seemed to catch on. These were fleabag rooms; The Lonely Bug was no normal motel. More than anything, I was grateful I didn't have to worry about dealing with people while Harold was there.

Once I arrived back in front of Room 13, I unlocked the door and gave it a quick once over. The room was messy and disheveled, but there was nothing more disgusting than the contents of our house stewing inside.

It felt strange putting my child in a room where people were just murdered, but there wasn't exactly a plethora of alternatives for me to choose from. The room just happened to be the last one on the strip, and I needed him to be as far away from Felix as possible.

I removed him from the back of the wagon and closed the door. When I entered the room, a chill ran down my spine. I set Harold down on the ruffled comforter and turned to the bulky tube in front of the bed. I twisted the dial and fortunately landed on Harold's favorite show—Pinky and the Brain.

The more mutilated rats I found in the house, the more it started to make sense. Maybe it wasn't good that he was so obsessed with it. Either way, I didn't have time to dissect him psychologically at the moment. I just needed to keep him distracted. I hoped the cartoon would do the trick.

"Mommy will be back in a little, okay?"

Harold stared mindlessly at the pair of comical rats.

I snatched the 'Do Not Disturb' handle and placed it on the doorknob just in case. But before I could leave, I heard a grumbling.

Harold cleared his throat like a seven-year smoker and said, "I love you, Mommy."

Immediately, my eyes welled up; it was the first time in his entire life that Harold told me that he loved me. Things were getting better. Daniel may have left us, but he doesn't see that Harold wants to be good. He wants to be normal.

I could barely get the words out… I was overcome by the emotion behind his loving gesture. I composed myself and replied, "I love you too, sweetie."

THE CHEMICAL GATEWAY

Tina staggered up around the back of The Lonely Bug to the rear bathroom window of the room she was prepared to die in. She'd already made the decision hours after being administered Greg's tainted blood. She wasn't going to become Dutch's meth zombie, and she wasn't going to wait for the HIV to bloom and slowly shut her down. She was done with life.

Tina had crushed the meth into a fine powder form and already sent a few shots up her nasal cavity. Her heart was thrashing about like a caged rabid dog inside her sternum. She was feeling more hyper than normal, and seeing entities and shapes that seemed to stretch her perception of reality. She felt paranoid about her surroundings, but the lust for violence was burning inside her—an alien feeling she'd never previously been capable of.

She moved an old trashcan in front of the window, which looked like the portal to another dimension. The wavy rectangular box moved like a mouth comprised of melting white flesh. She wanted to be eaten, she wanted to find the next spectrum of life, but first, she needed to conclude the current one.

As she stepped atop the nasty bin, Tina's dark paranoia preached to her. She looked back into her purse to ensure she had the rest of the meth and the hunting knife she'd lifted from the Army Navy store down the road. She required it to open the floodgates and allow her tainted life force to purge and run dry.

Irrespective of the horror and trepidation inside her, the crystal was doing what she hoped it might—allotting her the willpower to snuff herself out. While she was fearful, there was also a certain level of excitement inside her that thirsted to be done with the cruel world that had chewed her up and spat her out. Luckily, the window was still unlocked. She pulled it sideways and looked down. The fall looked neverending, like examining a bottomless pit in the reflection of a funhouse mirror.

The combination of shaky seating and her equilibrium feeling funky sent her unintentionally head-first into the bathroom. The landing couldn't have been more awkward; her cranium was the first part of her body to make contact below. The upper area of her tweaking skull and side of her face cracked against the yellowed rim of the porcelain toilet. The force of the fall shut her off and left a trail of blood leaking from her head and out of her ear.

Tina's purse fell in front of her and out spilled the partially opened baggie of meth. The stolen oversized black steel blade scraped across the tile before finally screeching to a stop right next to it.

The loud noise drew Harold's attention away from his vermin heroes (or villains). He plopped down off of the bed and onto the carpet and trotted around the corner, oozing an adolescent curiosity.

The bathroom door was already open, but the scene was not like anything he could've imagined. The bloody woman was intriguing, but the baggie of strange powder that was on the floor drew him in first.

Was it candy? Was it sugar? Vera wasn't able to find a spare moment to feed Harold breakfast amid the morning commotion. So, as he stuck his fat hand into the bag and palmed a generous handful of the woman's snack, he had no qualms about dropping the pungent powder into his mouth and swallowing it.

Harold was overcome with a strange chemical feeling and taste that stuck to his tongue. He looked at the woman's bleeding and unconscious body, and the big knife on the floor beside her. An odd anxiousness overwhelmed him as his ticker began to smack about in his chest madly.

The nervousness made him want to jump out of his own skin and forced him to exit the bathroom. He returned to his place on the bed and tried to focus on the silly lab rats that he enjoyed so much.

Despite the discomfort his body felt, Harold was still able to lose himself in the television. He ignored the sensations to the best of his ability, but after about fifteen minutes had amassed, the innocent cartoon had run its course, and more importantly, so had the meth.

The sounds of women screaming began to slowly raise around him; sprouting from a nearly inaudible level all the way up to a Spinal Tap 11. And while auditory hallucinations serenaded his eardrums, the visual ones latched onto the environment around him.

The walls shook like an earthquake was afoot, the wavy boundaries of the lined paneling slithered like wooden serpents, and the multi-colored mash of imagery strewn on the front of the television puked outward with the ferocity of a spaceship rocket thrust.

Darkness encapsulated the space around Harold until his scary world was only shadows. Until it was only one particularly massive shadow that stood on the side of him.

The strange man's enormous gut was bigger than any Harold had ever seen. He was balding on top but the hair that draped off the sides of his head was so long, it dangled at the back of his kneecaps. His dingy shirt and sweatpants were stained with the rancid emissions of his foul vessel. Not only could Harold see him and hear his heavy breathing amid the feminine screams, but he could also smell him.

The scent, while repugnant to the greater populous, didn't have the same effect on Harold. In fact, he actually enjoyed it. There was something about the bizarre man that was eerily familiar, and when the obese bastard finally unleashed a grin, things started to click in Harold's broken brain. He could plainly see the same bizarre bumblebee decay that had attached itself to his own enamel also plagued the man that stood before him…

Was this the man that Mommy and Daddy were arguing about all the time? Was this his *real* father?

The question remained unanswered in the simple space between Harold's ears. But one thing was certain, whoever this man was, he wanted to guide him.

The excited grunts that rattled off from The Slob's mouth were accompanied by a river of frothy drool. He waved Harold over back toward the bathroom, and the boy obeyed his command. Tina was still bleeding on the gnarly bath tile below, but that wasn't the focus, yet…

He pointed down to the blade on the ground excitedly, like a sporty father teaching his boy to pick up a baseball bat. Harold looked at the thick handle and grinned.

Once the weighty knife found Harold's palm, the nasty man got behind Tina's bleeding body and wrapped his grungy finger around the follicles at the top of her scalp. He pulled up on the hair, tightening the skin over her forehead, and traced over the top of her hairline.

"Right here," he grunted.

Harold slowly took hold of the clump of hair as a flood of drool dribbled around his lips. There was a hunger like he'd never felt suddenly growing inside of him.

Harold got down on his knees and carefully burrowed the razor-sharp edge into Tina's scalp and sunk it into her hairline. As the blood started to rush out, Harold pulled back hard on the hair and the pinkish meat underneath became exposed. He tried ripping it back but it wasn't ready, so instead, he continued to slice back and forth like a seesaw occupied by a pair of giddy children.

Suddenly, Tina's eyes sprung open. The blade must have struck a nerve that was more powerful than the blow that had incapacitated her. She tried to move her body and pull away, but her frame wasn't quite ready to cooperate with her stupefied brain.

Harold looked to the repulsive man for guidance. The Slob's eyes widened and he pointed to her throat and facial area. Harold nodded as Tina contorted her body and got to her knees by bridging herself up against the bathtub.

The first stab wasn't quite where Harold had intended it; he was thrusting upward, which caused the point of the blade to pierce her right cheek and then drove it a few inches further into the roof of her mouth.

When Harold yanked the knife out, her tongue got in the way. Upon exit, he left a split down the side of it that nearly reached the center, and only further stretched the limits of the hole in her cheek. Her mouth was closed, yet her crimson molars were on show.

The Slob pointed to her neck sternly, "No talking!" he yelled at Harold, upset with his placement.

Before Tina could think to react, Harold dove upward and sunk the knife-edge into her throat. The momentum of the vault saw his savage tackle send them both tumbling backwards into the tub. The energy of the fall sent the blade clean through and out the back of Tina's neck.

With the jugular vein being sliced through entirely, the blood outburst was incredible. The fountain-worthy flow could've garnered a few nickels and pennies, and judging by the horrified expression on Tina's face, she would've wished to meet the reaper as quickly as possible.

But Harold wasn't done, now it was time for the real fun to begin. He raised the unforgiving metal tip up with both of his meaty mitts wrapped around the handle, and brought it crashing down through her eye socket.

He looked over toward his twisted mentor who mimed an action, suggesting that he should apply his full body weight to sink it in deeper. Harold leaned into her harder, and the metallic murder weapon descended deeper as the sound of slick crunching humanity filled his ear canals.

He twisted the knife sideways and pulled slightly upward as he extracted it from her face. The wet red drizzled down over the catastrophic wound. Caught on the body of the blade sat Tina's 'good' eye.

Harold looked over toward his nefarious mentor—the flabby-cheeked fatso made a primal chewing motion and then nodded his head while continuing the action. Harold smiled and nodded back at the blurry bizarre man and raised the stained knife up to his mouth.

The chewy eye quickly slipped off the shiv as Harold manipulated it with his lips and tongue. He crushed down on the oily cornea and excitedly shredded it until he could feel the moist blood vessels wedging themselves between his tar-toned teeth.

The Slob watched on like any proud father passing down the traditions of their bloodline. When Harold looked into his eyes, he noticed something that felt unexpected—they were glossy. Emotion was something he hadn't expected to see in such a heartless entity.

Tina had stopped screaming, but the paranormal cries that showed themselves when the gross man appeared still carried on raging in Harold's head. They begged him to stop, but he didn't feel like listening to them.

Instead, he looked back toward The Slob who was happy to show him the next step. This hellish wisdom was guiding him along just fine. It was allowing him to discover and unpack the things embedded in his carnal code. The things that he hadn't understood until that very moment.

The Slob had repositioned himself appropriately and took a seat on the toilet. His gargantuan gut rested on his thighs as he locked eyes with Harold again. He lifted up his dirty digits and pointed at his belly, motioning up and down.

Harold again nodded, understanding who he was; the morbid curiosities that he'd been destined to explore, but previously had little comprehension of.

First, Harold cut through Tina's trashy clothing. It took him a few moments to find the proper areas to split the garments that would allow her body to be exposed to him. Once her saucy wet shell was uncovered in its entirety, Harold grew beyond excited.

Next, the knife slashed from the middle point of Tina's modest breasts, all the way down to the stubble of her bush. The freshly sharpened steel made pulling her mid-section apart and creating a door to her organs a child's task.

Tina's uterus, intestines, liver, and stomach had all shown themselves to Harold. The burning question of what was housed inside of the living people that surrounded him was beginning to be answered. It was an interest he'd had for some time in his malformed mind, but never one he was capable of remembering consistently. But now that it sat before him, he felt an evil enlightenment caress the cockles of his heartbeat.

He shoved the knife into her uterus with a casual nature of a hungry man sitting down to a steak dinner. He sliced it diagonally, severing one of the fallopian tubes and ovaries with the uterus meat.

"Ha! Ohhhhh!" The Slob laughed, then released a sigh of proudness after.

Harold adored the encouragement; he'd never received anything of that nature from a male figure before. Never mind one he so obviously connected with.

"Mouuuuth is good," The Slob continued.

The young secret sadist was eager to sling the rubbery muscle and glandular cells into his mouth and get a feel for their unique textures.

As Harold bit down on the various elements of the gamey baby factory, he felt the stringy strips with his tongue. Eventually, after a few more chews, he found the ovary between his upper and lower jaw. Some liquid was juiced under the pressure as his enamel crushed down into the ovarian cortex, and then one layer further into the mushy medulla.

"Eh?" The Slob inquired, asking him what he thought in his own primitive manner.

"Yum," Harold happily responded.

The massive maniac leaned over. Harold watched as his wavy arm reached into the bathtub and motioned toward the upper organs in Tina's petite cavity.

Harold used the handle of the blade to smash into the protective mortal encasement. After nearly a dozen swings and stabs, Tina's ribcage was broken enough for him to attempt to gain entry.

He placed his bloody hand on Tina's mutilated liver, and then quickly looked up at his teacher for further instruction. The Slob's lard insulated mug turned left to right three times, and then he pointed downward deeper.

Harold's hairy hand slipped behind the still-quivering repeatedly punctured liver and onto the stomach. Again, he looked to the fuzzy deviant being for confirmation. Harold could tell by the wicked leer that laid over the man's mouth that he was in the right place.

He stabbed through the tissue at the top of the stomach, slicing the esophagus clean through. Harold angled the blade at the base of the stomach next, but The Slob interjected.

"Eh! Wait!" he barked.

Harold had assumed he would be eating her gut next, but he had assumed wrong. Something else was on the horizon—another tool for the box. The slob remained with his hand outstretched, then slowly stood up from the toilet seat. The beastly man pulled down his spotted and stained sweatpants, exposing himself entirely.

His enormous scrotum looked familiar to Harold—his own body mirrored the ghastly disproportionate penis to balls ratio. The Slob's fingernails were nearly non-existent. Bitten down to the cuticle, he used the gritty nail tip to scratch at his puny shaft and attempted to arouse himself. He used his index finger and thumb on his other hand to form a circle, then impatiently entered it with all three-and-a-half inches of his haggard hunk.

The hardness of the meatpole had tightened so tensely that the overfilled sores that peppered his penis spewed outward like curdled milk being squished through a spaghetti strainer. The Slob's eyes spread as the foul bumpy paste clumped up all over the hand he was fucking. The emerald tinge manufactured within the barf-worthy creamy secretion looked like it was radioactive.

Harold watched on in amazement. He'd never seen the body grow or release anything that color before; it was like magic in his corrupt mutant mind. He plunged the knife back into Tina's face to serve as a resting place. Then Harold unzipped his jeans and quickly peeled them off in seconds, hungry to emulate his otherworldly idol and try his own hand at growing.

Harold removed his miraculously unsoiled diaper next and set it down beside his pants. He then formed a circle with his fingers while he attempted to stimulate himself with the other hand. As his pitiful pointer crawled out of his wrinkly flesh cave, a loud grunt erupted from behind him. It was a grunt of discontent… a grunt of intended guidance.

When Harold turned back to understand the reason for getting his attention, he saw the sick man pointing at Tina's still-attached stomach that Harold had dropped amid his excitement to strip down. But The Slob was pointing at the gastroesophageal junction that remained severed at the top of the stomach.

A mixture of bile, cum, and mostly-digested pork-fried rice comprised the thick and uneven brownish mush that was seeping out of the junction.

SON OF THE SLOB

Harold lifted up her stomach with his free hand and aligned his tiny pecker with the sloppy hole. Once the head of his dick made its way inside the hole on the top of Tina's stomach, he set his free hand on the other side of the frothing food basket.

He moved the organ back and forth along with his hips, ramming his erection as deep as he could into the soft porridge contained inside the flesh bag. The shudder-worthy putrid last meal erupted around his pubic region and made a wet squishy sound as he pumped it harder.

"Yes… yesssss…" The Slob mumbled.

Harold focused on the fuzzy elements of the meth rush that was still distorting his vision. The stomach looked like a hole that led to hell, and he was quickly realizing he enjoyed the bedlam. The wailing depraved moans that echoed from the lips of the destroyed women he pictured in his brain raised his sensual sensitivities beyond imagination.

He felt the foreign feeling begin to stir inside him. It was as if there was so much exhilaration and utter elation brewing, that it needed to rip its way out of his disgusting body. Harold began to tremble, his pelvic region bucking like he was trying to ride a feisty stallion.

He didn't see the orgasmic essence exit, but he felt it. The culmination of his horrific perversion and necrophiliac sleaze slaughter were like a Christmas gift that had been sitting under the tree since he was born. Finally, the devil's donation had been utilized.

Harold let the impregnated digestive sack slip away from his fingers and slumped over onto the side of the tub. While there was a strangeness running through his body, the toxic glass still twinkled inside him.

The Slob looked on like a weight had been lifted off of his hallucinogenic shoulders—his boy could swim with the sharks. While he oozed with honor and ghastly glee, there was still a part of the ritual that had been previously interrupted. He took his pus-clad index finger and aimed it at Tina's partially parted hairline.

Harold, not truly exhausted yet, pushed himself forward and reached for the knife that was still stuck in Tina's pretty little face. He grabbed at the handle and rocked it from side to side before ripping upward and finally dislodging it from her sad excuse for a skull.

His hairy hand then wrapped around her blood-soaked matted follicles as he buried the blade deep into the top of her head. He scooted forward toward the front of the tub so that, as he cut further down into her scalp, he could simultaneously peel the top of her head off.

The wet ripping of her flesh sounded like blood being slurped through a straw in an almost empty cup, mixed with cheap fabric being pulled apart. The slimy trail of red dissipated slowly as the many sappy lines of liquid were stretched upon the damp scalp being separated from the exposed glistening dome underneath.

The Slob's fat sweaty hands clapped slowly in adoration; this was truly a sensational scalping. But after the praise had been heaped, it was onto the next step—tasting upon a treat for the ages... a delicacy of the delinquent minded. He took his sausage finger and tracked around a small portion; maybe a sixth of Tina's scalp.

Harold sliced and separated the chunk from the greater collective. He then took the appalling wad, hair first, and stuck it inside his mouth. There was no amount of chewing that would make the gristly skin and awkward hair easily edible. So, once he'd collected enough saliva in his mouth, just as he'd done with the ashes at Eve's house, and the mother rat back home, he balled up the contents and swallowed.

Something about ingesting Tina's head made Harold feel a calmness overcome his attitude. Despite his rapidly pumping heart, sweat-soaked skin, and a constant sense that vomit might erupt from him at any moment, the vibes were good. Even though his brain couldn't sort it out, the nausea he was on the verge of was from the meth in his system, not the countless atrocious acts he'd committed or the parts of Tina he'd ingested.

As Harold's tiny fat gut rumbled relentlessly, he looked back to The Slob to calm him. He focused on the adoration that still lingered in his eyes, and the foul fondness they had for each other. The bond that they had built in such a short period was something that would last a lifetime. Even if they never saw each other again…

A RECURRING NIGHTMARE

As I was exiting Room 7, a terrible feeling wormed its way inside me. I couldn't help but worry and wonder how long Harold could remain entertained by the television set. With each room I'd finished clearing out, I considered checking on him.

I kind of was... after every few minutes of cleaning, I returned to the entrance and looked down the strip toward the car and Room 13. The door remained closed and the "Do Not Disturb" handle hanger remained intact. He had to be fine, there was nothing in the room that could hurt him, and no other way out but the front door.

Still, it didn't make me feel any better. It had been nearly three hours now, and while I was happy that he hadn't come running out of the room screaming, I couldn't help but fear the worst. I suppose it's just what I do these days.

The uncomfortable lump in my throat and the empty feeling of bottomlessness in the pit of my stomach was taking hold of me. I felt compelled to check on him—I couldn't clean another inch until I did.

As I wheeled my cleaning cart back out and closed the door, I glanced back toward the office. Felix had finally come around; his wide sticky fingers were glued to the pornographic pages of a scummy new special edition of 'Jugs Magazine.'

He was awake but thankfully distracted. But I knew his attention span was just like his personality—short and crude. I needed to keep things moving, but more importantly, I needed to check on Harold and this nagging fucking feeling that felt too intense to casually pass over.

I power-walked my way up to the room and slowly opened the door. The television was still on, but the dent atop the comforter where Harold had been seated was vacant. An eerie feeling of petrification knocked the air out of me. It was hard to say exactly why, but my maternal instincts had never screamed out in such a manner.

It's probably fine, he's just using the bathroom. That's all, there's literally nothing else to do in this room, I rationalized with myself.

"Harold?" I called out.

I took a step closer toward the bathroom. I tried to listen deeper, hoping he would respond to me. But beyond the childish noise coming from the kid's show on the TV, there wasn't much to be heard… except for a faint scraping noise. What could it possibly be?

I took another step closer to the door and the metallic grinding slightly intensified. *What on Earth is that noise?* I wondered, not daring to answer the question with my own macabre imagination. *Why do I feel this way? I feel like I'm going to have a heart attack. Something's definitely wrong, oh God, what has he done? What has Harold done?*

The feeling was overwhelming. Long ago, I'd learned that intuition is a real thing. And that blaring level of profound awareness and acute sensitivity was something that I hadn't felt in a long time. Since I was trapped in that house of horrors all those years ago. It was a feeling that I prayed never to witness again. It was my only aspiration really, in the grand scheme of things.

The door was cracked open slightly but the angle and minute sliver that exposed what laid behind it left just about everything to the imagination. As I carefully pushed the door forward, I quickly realized that even my damaged mind couldn't have prepared me for what I was about to see...

Harold sat with his pants removed, in the bathtub, with what looked to be a woman's mutilated body. My vantage point allowed me to take in all the gory details—the cracked open chest cavity, the ripped and destroyed internal organs, the face carved beyond all recognition, and, maybe most frighteningly of all, the missing scalp.

Flashes flew into my brain—snapshots of the sickening contents of The Slob's house, and the collection turned factory line of young girls mutilated inside of it. The ghoulish permanent grin etched into the face of the woman I'd been confined inside with.

I hadn't thought about Sandra in some time, she seemed like such a sweet person. I'd done my damnedest to try and save her, but that was far from good enough. As I stared at the woman's shiny bare scalp, I couldn't help but recall hers. The deep rawness of the unearthed tissue, and the patches of exposed skull would make most ordinary folks feel sick, but there was nothing normal about my human trajectory.

I had seen it all before and then some. While I felt fear, and shock, and disdain, maybe the most glaring feeling of the gamut was somehow disappointment.

When you've had your face destroyed, your fetus bashed to mush, and have been vaginally assaulted in the most nefarious manner, you become a smidge deadened on the inside. The deceased woman in the tub just fostered a numbness that spanned my entire body. The prioritization of my emotional totem pole had been twisted and bent beyond recognition, just like everything else in my life.

When my eyes reached Harold, I couldn't help but be reminded of his father. The woman's intestines were tangled around his body, and her blood was stuck to various parts of him and his clothing. He'd seen fit to remove one of her ribs and sat grinding his rotten teeth against each side of it.

I remained speechless and inside my own head, trying to understand exactly what the fuck had happened. *Who was the woman with the massive knife still stuck inside her face? Did she just come in the room randomly? Why did she bring a knife?*

Suddenly, I noticed there were some items by my feet. I was able to pull my vision away from the carnage and looked down at the spilled bag of powder on the ground and disheveled handbag. Something about it looked familiar. I grabbed hold of it and flipped it over to reveal a deep red embroidered heart sitting in the center of it.

Clarity ensued and I quickly gazed upon the girl's blood-drenched outfit, which now looked familiar as well. *Tina? What the fuck are you doing here?* I wondered.

My heart started to ache just like the one on her purse. Something must have happened to her; it didn't make any sense why she would be back here with a smaller portion of the drugs and a knife. Maybe I just didn't know her as well as I thought. Maybe she had been lying to me?

I examined Harold again, in search of answers that might lead me to an understanding. Amid the blood and pieces of the poor girl that were splattered all over his face, I saw something else. As he gnawed on the bone like a manic mutt, I saw the meth powder. It left a coating of dust on his nose and cheeks that still had yet to be overcome by the blood smears.

Harold's behavior was always eccentric, but the manner of his movements had been altered. The speed at which he was moving was different—it was like someone else was controlling him and had hit the fast-forward button. He was high as a fucking kite.

There was no way for me to know exactly what had happened, but there were two things that I felt I knew with a relative certainty. First, what had happened in Room 13 wasn't masterminded by Harold, it was the result of Tina breaking back into the room. And second, Harold didn't deserve to be punished as a result of her reckless actions.

"What happened, sweetie?" The words came out of my mouth but I didn't really expect an answer to spawn upon asking the question.

Harold continued biting down on the bone ferociously, if nothing else, it seemed to distract him. My mind was starting to race; *what the fuck am I gonna do?!*

If I called the police, Harold would be shipped away somewhere—locked inside an experimental facility to rot. Was that a bad thing? It would serve as an escape for me (and Daniel if he ever decided to return).

I looked at his yellow eyes; despite the drug-fueled saucer-sized pupils polluting his expression, there was still an innocence bound to them. Harold was a child that never had a chance, and part of that was because I hadn't given him one. The non-genetic half of the ailments that were eating through his chances of success fell hard on my own tired shoulders.

In many ways, I was facing the same conundrum that my mother had. Would I choose my own life and happiness, or help someone who was sick find their way? My mother could never live with the guilt of leaving her disturbed daughter, Lisa, to her own devices. Neither could I.

However, as if my guilt and feeling of obligation wasn't enough, another frightening question popped into my head. *Am I legally responsible for any of this?* There were many other questions I had that attached to that one, but I started to think about Felix and the other rooms. If I didn't make a decision damn soon, someone else would be making the decision for me.

"Stay here, don't touch or do anything! Okay?" Again, there was no response and Harold continued his teething.

I raced out of the room and closed the door behind me. Then I headed back down the strip and into the office.

Felix was still parked behind the counter, distracted by the pair of tits he was drooling over on the magazine page. When I entered the office, as usual, he couldn't help but make conversation.

"Hey there, beautiful, how many rooms are ready?"

"I just finished up with number seven, but some of the others might need a little extra love… I figured since you got the new carpet cleaner that I could do half of the rooms today and the other half tomorrow? Does that sound okay to you?" I asked, hoping to avoid elongating our exchange.

"These fuckin' junkies don't need to feel like they're checking into a five-star resort, don't go too crazy, I'm sure they'll fuck it up again in no time."

"Right, I just figured a once-over would be nice, get some of the vomit and spilled booze out of the rugs. Maybe it'll help with the smell… but if anyone wants to check in early, you've still got seven rooms ready to go," I explained while extracting the Bissell from the rear closet.

Felix looked up from the magazine and squinted his eyes; my enthusiasm was probably a bit out of left field for him, but not enough to raise a red flag. He saw my initial reaction to the machine, and probably found it curious how I could be so anxious to leverage it again.

"Just as long as you know your pay don't change any…" he mumbled, returning his bloodshot eyes to the porno magazine.

Brilliant. If it didn't empty his pockets any extra, he could give a shit less. This was the precise reaction I was hoping to garner from the shrewd owner.

"Understood," I replied, dragging the vacuum back out the front door.

En route back to the room, I slyly began to push my cleaning cart with me alongside the vacuum. I couldn't help but stealthily glance back and keep my eyes in Felix's direction. He still had his gaze glued to the page as I trudged forward. I slipped back into Room 13 without Felix or anyone else taking notice.

Once I closed the door, I locked it. As I stripped off my outfit and shoes, I felt sick. I was unable to comprehend the scene that I was about to be intimately familiar with.

I was already starting to calculate the horrors that I would need to partake in to make this mess go away. As I entered the bathroom again, I saw Harold was still trying to chew down to the bone marrow. He remained in a seated position on Tina's pelvic region like when I left.

I was grateful that most of the gory happenings had transpired in the bathtub. It would make for a fast clean-up, which was exactly what I needed. The Bissell was really only going to be required to pull up the pooled blood that had sunken into the green bath mats that surrounded the toilet and front of the tub.

It looked like Harold's jeans had been kicked off, but there was still a healthy amount of crimson that had saturated them. After I fired up the Bissell and finished sucking the rugs clean, I tried the same on his jeans. The end result wasn't perfect, but the natural navy-blue tone of the pants camouflaged much of the still splotchy areas.

I set the jeans on the towel rack to dry and then scurried over to my cleaning cart to retrieve a few of the black garbage bags. I looked at the gigantic hunting knife that sat buried between where her eyes used to be.

What the fuck am I doing? I can't get out of this without… without… cutting her into pieces, I thought.

I looked back at Harold in aggravation and disgust. He seemed to return a similar gaze. He'd never seen me naked, which must be uncomfortable. It wasn't as if he hadn't seen enough abnormal views, what would one more hurt?

As I continued to stew in my loathsome judgements, I couldn't help but think that Harold was not the entire problem, but still a massive part of it. Was watching his nude mother dismember a hooker's corpse going to help him?

I imagined, in some way, that hiding Tina's body and forgetting this horrific episode ever transpired would afford him another chance at life. But my gory endeavor would only serve to baste his broken brain in more violence and depravity—something he seemed to circumstantially have more than enough of already.

While Tina deserved a proper burial and send-off, she was already dead; that much wasn't changing. But I quickly realized I would need to transform her corpse into a transportable form, and eliminate the chance of the deed being discovered before worrying about her memorial.

I couldn't believe I was doing it again; it was like the worst recurring nightmare was looping into my daydreams, slumber, and reality. As my fingers curled around the handle of the blade and I dislodged it, I couldn't help but try to justify it over and over to myself.

He was drugged. Tina drugged Harold, and this is what happens when you don't take your opportunity and exit. You end up dead in a shitty motel room, you end up raising hell for others...

I resented Tina returning after everything I'd done for her. I put my ass on the line letting her come back. I shared my dark moments with her, I wished for her to heal, to take the one fucking opportunity she had and go. But somehow, my good intentions have led me to dismembering her mutilated carcass.

I can't fucking win, I thought as I straightened her arm out and began to saw through the area nearest to her shoulder. *Thank goodness for this knife, I'm not sure how I'd transport her otherwise...*

It was like the knife was crafted with a refined crudeness that allowed it to cut through flesh and bone like fabric. It felt so casual initially to my numb psyche, but when I laid eyes on the tree-like interior that displayed the various layers of the limb, without warning, I lost it.

Thankfully, the toilet was right beside me and the seat had been left up when the vomit blast came. I hadn't had anything for breakfast, so it was mostly just a watery acidic fluid that was squirting down and discoloring the pool of clear water. Once I was finally able to pause my upheaval, I controlled my breathing as best I could.

I knew time was of the essence and tried to pause my sickness. Then I quickly recalibrated my thoughts and put the pressure back on myself. If I didn't find a way to get through this in exponential fashion, I'd have far worse issues to deal with than analyzing my own morality.

I leaned the severed arm up against the edge at the front of the tub and allowed the blood to rush outward down the drain. Getting as much out as I could to make it less messy and easier for me to transport.

Harold watched closely, eyes bulging, still somberly suckling upon Tina's detached rib while I sawed through her other shoulder. I was able to sever it nearly as easily as the first, and subsequently lined it up uniformly.

The legs were a little more difficult because of their positioning and where Harold was seated. I cut slowly and carefully in an effort to avoid accidentally gashing him. A few squishy slices later, the legs were lined up right beside her arms. It looked quite bizarre, but as I watched the flood of crimson dispel from the four limbs and rush down the drain, I felt I was getting closer to completing the distressing endeavor.

Cutting off Tina's head wasn't as difficult as I thought it might be for two reasons—the bodily reason being that it appeared Harold had already stabbed through a third of her throat during his rampage. And the ethical reason being that one of her eyes had been removed entirely and the other was bludgeoned to an unrecognizable pulp. This helped me disconnect the humanity from her destroyed vehicle. I didn't feel good about it, but it had to be done.

I turned on the water and pressed down on the body numerous times. Then I applied as much compression to the limbs as my physique allowed. It took me a few minutes to get out as much blood as I could from the parts and down the drain. Once I felt satisfied, I turned off the shower-head. The next step would be bagging her. I had to do it carefully; I reasoned that whatever I was holding her inside of needed to be tidy. I couldn't be dragging the mess outside.

I opened the first garbage bag as wide as I could, and then mustered all of my vigor. I slipped Tina's petite torso inside, but of course, there were some drippings that lingered down the side of the bag. I used some of the toilet tissue to dry the exterior before opening up a second bag on the floor outside the tub. I spread it as wide as I could and slowly dropped her wrapped torso inside.

I repeated the double-bagging technique one more time to safely store her four tiny limbs and head. Those were far easier because I was able to accurately drop them right in without drizzling blood on the exterior. I rinsed off the bloody blade in the sink, then wrapped it in a towel and triple bagged it separately. I didn't want it cutting through or opening up one of the other bags of Tina's parts.

I picked the powdered crystal meth off the floor. I shook my head and flushed the remainder down the toilet. Before tying up the second bag that contained her limbs and head, I remembered there was still one piece of her that hadn't been disposed of yet.

I reached toward Harold to snatch the rib bone he'd been infatuated with away from him. He growled like a junkyard dog and then snapped at me. Harold still appeared to be in the firm grip of the shit Tina had served up to him. Instead of fighting with him, I joined him.

First, I peeled off the gray sweater that he was still wearing. He didn't enjoy me taking it off of him, but he wasn't enraged at it either. There was no way that I was getting the blood out. The thing looked like a butcher had worn it for a week straight. I balled it up and then tossed it into the same bag as the knife.

I stepped into the shower and turned the water on. The hot steam felt splendid and served as a minor distraction from the horrors I was entangled within. I snapped back into clean-up mode and washed both of us spotless. As the remainder of Tina's blood swirled down the drain, I tried not to think about her too much. When she left, I really thought she had a chance. It was a shame.

Harold had somehow managed to remain docile while I straightened up the murder scene. It had taken a decent amount of time, but not too much. But if we hung around and overstayed our welcome, there was no telling if Felix might come pounding on the door at any moment.

Once I dried us off, I redressed us as fast as possible. Now I needed to get the pieces of Tina into the hatch of the wagon. Harold found his way in front of the television again and continued to suck on the bone. The attachment was like a baby to a pacifier—it was keeping him calm and quiet.

I opened the door to the outside and looked around the parking lot; it was still as empty as it was when we'd arrived. Shifting my focus back to the office, it was also empty. Felix was either asleep, on the couch, or taking a dump. Either way, I needed to get the body out fast before he decided that he felt like reappearing.

I opened the hatch of the wagon and was happy to see, amid the clutter, a large blanket that we'd used for picnics in the past. The far distant past...

I hoisted up each of the black bags and slid them inside, one by one. Each time I checked to see if Felix had returned, he thankfully hadn't. Once they were all in the back, I slipped the cover over the top of the bags and then closed the hatch.

Despite the dreadful feeling of knowing I needed to get the fuck out of there right away, I couldn't. I knew I needed to spend a few minutes at least making the beds and removing the trash from the other rooms, otherwise, Felix might catch on that something was amiss.

After locking Harold in Room 13, I completed the remaining work as speedily as possible. I noticed that a few patrons had made their way into the lower numbered rooms as I pushed the cleaning cart and the Bissell back into the office. Felix was nowhere to be found at the moment. I was sure he couldn't be far, but escaping without another exchange would have been a dream come true. I hurried to put things into their place before shutting the closet door.

When I turned back to the front of the office, I was greeted by the jingle of the entrance door swinging open. Crossing the threshold was about the last person I was hoping to see that day—Detective Wells.

"Vera, you never called," he said, tipping his hat backward and allowing his eyes to engage me.

His presence popping in so quickly, and my general nerves regarding the dastardly deed I'd just partaken in, caused me to jump.

"Oh! Detective Wells," I yelped. "Geeze! You can't sneak up on me like that!" I laughed jokingly. It was the only approach I thought worked. "I-I haven't called because nothing's happened. At least that I've seen. You'd have to talk to Felix to hear about the evenings, though… I'm only here during the mornings and sometimes afternoons…"

I was rambling on far too much. The stone-cold and cool demeanor I'd initially introduced myself to him with had all but evaporated. He must've felt like he was speaking with a different person. I needed to calm down fast.

He squinted his eyes at me, "Is your hair wet?" he asked.

"What?" I heard the question clear as day, but I had no answer to explain it. It wasn't raining outside, I had clearly been here for some time, so why the fuck was my hair wet? Detective Wells was an observant, nosy prick.

"It's a simple question, Vera, is your hair wet?"

"Well, it's not wet per se, I tried a new mousse, it's supposed to give your hair that wet look." It was a damn good lie.

"Ah, I get it. It really does the trick. Say, you know, my wife was wanting to do something just like that actually, what's the name of the magical mousse, if you don't mind me asking?"

He had me now, "I really don't remember, to be honest, but since you seem to be popping in around here so much, I'll make a note for the next time I see you."

"Gee, that'd be swell, Vera. I'm sure our paths will be crossing again." His cocky smile shined true.

I could tell he enjoyed toying with me, but I wasn't sure exactly why. I could have given a shit less, up until a few hours ago. But now that there was a dead girl in the hatch of my vehicle maybe sixty yards from where we stood, I felt far less confident about jabbing him back.

"Oh, and one other thing. One of my undercover informants got us a little information on the case. He says that there's a prostitute named Tina Sparks who might be tangled up in the murders. She was working for the guy that got stabbed in the room."

Wells extracted a photo of Tina that was a few years older. Her innocent smile and kind eyes made her look like she had such a promising future. The face I'd just finished looking at on the head I had decapitated told a different tale.

"The picture is a little old, but have you seen this girl or heard her name mentioned around here at all?"

"No, but I'll keep my eyes open, and if I hear anything, I'll call you," I lied.

An unexpected wave of emotion hit me hard—a mixture of anxiety, regret, and grief lingered. I was trying to hold on. If I broke down, it would be the end of things without a doubt. I gritted my teeth and then pretended to sneeze.

"God bless you," Detective Wells said.

I turned away from him and back toward the front desk. I snatched a tissue and blew my nose while composing myself and secretly wiping the would-be tears from my eyes.

"Sorry, it gets dusty in those rooms sometimes." I wasn't lying, but I wasn't exactly telling the truth either.

"Yeah, I can imagine. Alright, that's all for today," Detective Wells said, opening the door beside him. "But remember, if you hear anything, even if you don't think it's important—"

"I'll call you," I said, complying one-hundred-percent.

After I watched Detective Wells drive out of the parking lot in his car, I immediately raced out of the office. I needed to move before Felix returned. I quickly snagged my coat out of my car and entered Room 13.

Thankfully, Harold was still staring at the television, nibbling at Tina's rib absentmindedly. I wrapped my coat around him, ushering him out of the room and into the backseat of the wagon. Once I started the engine, I never looked back.

AFTER THOUGHTS

I set the last bag of Tina's body parts in the basement. The only area where there was any room was where Harold had left the crucifix he'd constructed from his fecal matter and the collection of dead rats he'd accrued. I was too tired to clean it up, and I had more pressing things to ponder, like what was I going to do with Tina's quartered corpse. I needed to figure it out soon before the vermin got into it and made things even worse.

I removed Harold's sweater from the bag with the knife and moseyed over to the washing machine. I dumped in a surplus of stain-removing detergent, my own clothes, started the cycle, and hoped for the best.

After dressing myself, I headed upstairs and maneuvered around the piles of junk back over to Harold's room. When I opened the door, I couldn't help but start to sob.

I had no other choice but to subdue him. I felt terrible about tying him to the bed, but I didn't feel safe around him at the moment. He was quiet, but the chemicals that he'd ingested left a deranged fury floating around his pupils. Tomorrow would be better. Hopefully, the effects will be extinguished by that point.

It took me over an hour to get that fucking bone away from him. Now it sat in the bag downstairs, reintroduced to Tina's torso. I was frightened the entire time, I always assumed I knew what he was capable of, but seeing it is a completely different thing.

Things were beginning to fall apart rapidly, I needed to stop the momentum. I feel like I'm doing my best to reverse it considering some of the macabre steps I'd taken at The Lonely Bug. But how long could I keep this up?

Was this just a one-time event for Harold? My heart answered yes, but my mind wasn't so quick to draw that conclusion:

Heart: It was the drugs; Harold wasn't in control of himself.

Mind: Plenty of people take drugs and don't cut a stranger to pieces.

Heart: But he's just a child.

Mind: A child that does evil adult things…

Heart: What's to say he wasn't defending himself? Tina brought the meth and knife, what if she just went crazy?

Mind: What about the rats? They aren't humans, of course, but that showcases he has a very violent tendency, does it not?

Heart: I suppose it does, but he's never done anything that bad before, if he wasn't thrust into such a frightening situation, it would've been different.

Mind: Are you sure?

Heart: No…

Mind: You always defend him but this is a tough sell.

Heart: He's had a difficult life, all odds have always been against him. He just needs a chance to be better.

Mind: Maybe, but where do you draw the line? Apparently not at murder…

Heart: This is different, if there were no drugs involved, I would feel differently.

Mind: Do you really think he'll get better?

Heart: That's the only thing I can hope for.

My life was essentially just Harold. What was I going to do? Without him, I would just clean rooms and walk around with my ghastly face frightening those I came into contact with. Reliving my nightmares while I slept and praying to stray from them when I awoke.

It was a scary notion; my perception had been blurred. No sliver of my own personal life and singular being meant anything anymore. It was all a distant and defunct memory. Sure, I was a survivor, but what did that really mean? I had no idea where to go from here.

At least Harold gave me a purpose. Certainly, it was a dark and gruesome one, but it was a purpose nonetheless. Cleaning up after him is something I would do if I had to because, in my heart, I believe there is some decency inside him. My curse is that I feel like it's my responsibility to get it to shine through.

I closed Harold's door and, in unison, closed out the thoughts I'd been debating about him. But it didn't take me long to move onto the next topic.

I wish I just didn't have to think about anything for a moment, but there was too much going on. Was I going to just dump Tina in the ground in some unmarked grave? She herself told me that she had no one, if her body was discovered, would it even matter?

I internally shamed myself for asking such a fucked-up question. It made me feel cold-hearted.

In my head, I was now beginning to blame Daniel. If he hadn't left, I wouldn't have had to take Harold to work with me. He had abandoned us. I suppose that without his physical and financial help, this house of cards is going to come crashing down not too long from now.

The burden was back-breaking, I was almost excited by the thought of it all being over. As angry as I was, I knew deep down that it wasn't his fault. He'd put up with many years of stress and negativity. Despite the salty taste that he'd left stinging my mouth, I hoped that wherever he was, he was doing okay.

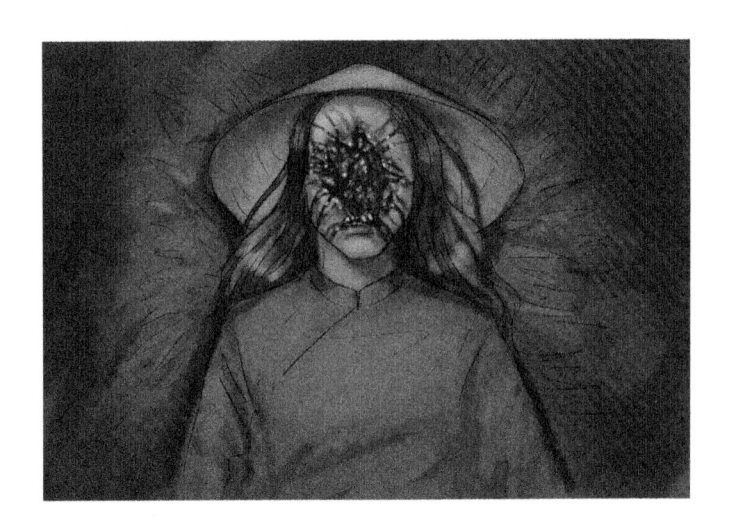

BACK IN THE BUSH

The vegetation was thicker than normal outside of the village. Their mud-caked faces were that of hell and hatred. Daniel understood why—their whole way of life had been disrupted and destroyed. The steaming bullet holes blown out through the bodies of their once functional loved ones was a harsh reality to be surrounded by.

Many were soldiers—Viet Cong pawns that aimed to see the American troops take their last breath, but some were just men and women that had been caught in the crossfire or mistaken for a threat.

Daniel stood over the body of one such woman. The bullet buried in her mouth had come from the barrel of his M16. She tried to speak, and as she choked on her blood, she managed to gurgle out a handful of emotional words that were indecipherable to Daniel.

He felt less than human as the final words of the poor woman's deathbed confession fell on his deaf (or at the very least, uneducated) ears. But suddenly, as the dying woman's hands slid down from her raw and distorted maw and approached her belly, Daniel began to understand. Due to her baggy attire and the horrifying hole in her face, he hadn't noticed it initially—the woman was pregnant.

As she shook violently and gave off a death rattle, Daniel locked in on the despair in her eyes as his own filled with tears. Her bloody curled hands and sharp fingernails lifted up her garment and exposed her rotund belly.

The mortal contents were throbbing wildly; it was almost as if the flesh nestled inside her womb understood what was going on. That its mother was transitioning to whatever came next before it had even gained an understanding of how things kicked off.

The thrashing became more absurd; the skin of her soft stomach stretched outward and pulled in many directions, elasticizing to unfathomable dimensions. The woman's gory pie-hole came together, bearing a sinister beam. The havoc on the right side of her face still left the top and bottom rows of teeth disconnected and dripping.

Daniel was losing his composure and looked around at the rest of the chaos that surrounded him. It was all pure madness, she was pure madness. His heart fluttered, adrenaline pumped, and he wondered how she could still be smiling. How the baby inside her could be so strong before it was born. He had no answers.

Daniel remained looming over her, trying to offer whatever small comfort a murderer could to their dying victim. *That's what I am, a murderer,* he thought to himself as tears continued to cloud his pupils.

Suddenly, the deranged woman plunged her fingers into her over-active abdomen. The screams that came from her voice box sounded different than the ones that encircled them on the battlefield. Peppered in between the constant gunfire, they never stopped, but hers sounded inhuman…

The uncomfortable wail continued to sound off as the woman's fingers tore through her own exterior. Daniel wanted to speak, to try and reason with her, but his mouth remained in a static state. It was like he'd looked directly into the eyes of Medusa.

The hole in her torso was gaping and overflowing with a gelatinous-like gist as her hand sunk further into her gut. Daniel wanted to scream, he wanted to run, but he was frozen in time. He was at the mercy of whatever unsettling imagery the woman could conjure up.

When the head came out, it was anything but what he'd expected. It was an impossible sight. The baby's slimy face wasn't that of Vietnamese origin. Its head was somehow hairy and balding at the same time. Its teeth were toned with black tar over their inceptual yellow core. A strange stubble, which shouldn't have been present until after decades of life had passed, dotted its wretched face. An odorous stench that paralleled the juice dripping out the ass end of a garbage truck on a hot summer day, unleashed itself from the womb.

It was Harold.

The same indolent and devious smile dominated his foul expression. The same natural obesity allowed the limits of his body to bulge fantastically. As Harold's neck worked its way out of her, Daniel noticed that there were many other heads flanking him. The rats were plump and deformed; they appeared like the ones Daniel had seen after Harold finished 'playing' with them.

Somehow, the vermin still found ability and movement. Despite their mashed and mauled vessels, the countless rats made their way out of the screaming woman's core in a state of frenzy. Chewing their way through the rubbery flesh, shrieking with a harsh distress and agony.

Regardless of the outpouring of rodents, the dying woman lifted Harold up further until his quivering body and abnormally shaggy hands were now visible. Between the sick boy's sausage fingers was a round, wet grenade. He held it as firmly as his newborn limbs allowed, then gleefully gazed upon Daniel in his mimic state of total terror.

"I'm for you," Harold managed to spout off.

As the mutilated rats ran up Daniel's legs and began to sink their teeth into his flesh, Harold pulled the pin from the grenade out and let the pineapple body drop down to the gore chasm below him.

The deranged rats bit hard into Daniel's body as the fiery explosion overtook everything around them. Daniel could feel the heat from the eruption coming at his face rapidly. The sweat mounted and dripped off of him until the inferno cloud blacked out every inch his eyes could see.

***

When Daniel awoke, the sweat beads had welled up enough to saturate his entire head. His scalp was so moist that it looked like he'd just stepped out of the shower. The release of salty water from his pores was so extreme that the couch cushion felt like it had just been soiled.

As his eyes adjusted to the darkness, a few murmurs of discomfort and fright escaped him. They didn't form any words, but it was the definition of what distress sounded like. Eventually, he focused on a figure sitting across the living room by the window.

The moonlight partially draped across Morris's stoic face and one of his bloodshot eyes. He didn't have to ask what was wrong. They both lived the same nightmare.

"That's why I don't really sleep much, Danny boy. They never quite go away, do they?" Morris asked rhetorically.

"I killed a woman. A pregnant woman," Daniel replied.

"Shit happens in the bush. You ain't the only one with bodies on your soul. Sometimes them people just didn't wanna get out of dodge. They hated us… we did everything we could to keep 'em intact. But sometimes there's just collateral damage. And sometimes, they just plain fuckin' deserve it."

"She didn't deserve it…" Daniel replied.

"You don't know that."

"What about the baby inside her that didn't even take its first breath? Did he fucking deserve it too?!" Daniel's voice escalated and he was now trembling like ocean waters.

"Maybe... if he was going to turn into one of them little mutha fuckas that run into a platoon with an uncorked grenade after a few years, then, yes! He deserved it! It's a war, Daniel! Just because it ain't in the papers and on the television no more don't mean it ain't still going on. The shit don't end... not for you, not for me, not for any damn one. The shit'll never end." Morris remained eerily still in the chair despite the unhinged passion he conveyed.

Daniel looked down and dragged himself closer to the arm of the couch to position himself to sit upright. Morris's views on the war weren't going to help him sort anything out. But maybe there were other questions his insights may serve a purpose in reviewing.

"Do you think that's why my baby was taken from me? Is that why Harold has found me? Because I killed that baby in Nam?" Daniel asked.

"Don't much believe in karma myself. Don't much believe in anything anymore, Danny. I'm not sure if all this is someone's plan or if the universe is random. But if this is all by design, boy..."

"What?" Daniel wondered.

"Would I like to airhole that mutha fucka when I see him. I'd watch him bleed out and feel absolutely nothing."

While his insights did little more for Daniel than highlight that life isn't fair, he felt that it was good for Morris to vent too. He was stuck in his dirty apartment, just alone with his thoughts. It was clear that he needed to talk too.

Morris approached the window and looked out in a paranoid fashion. His eyes scanned under the streetlight and darkness outside as if he was looking for someone.

"It never stopped, Danny boy. They still coming over here. Preparing. Waiting for the right moment. Half the fuckin' people in this country respect those gooks more than they do us. They get business at their little fuckin' restaurants, and what do we get? Spit on. We get spit on and tossed aside like garbage to rot away. I'll tell you what, though, I'll be ready. When the time comes, no goddamn one is getting the jump on me. And I'll be the first one to say I told you so."

"It's not like that, Morris. The people coming here now just want a better life. I'm lost just as much as you, maybe more, but I don't blame them. I don't know who to blame, but I don't blame them."

"You'll see. You'll fuckin' see," Morris muttered, still looking out the window and scanning the street.

Daniel wasn't in the mood to debate the war or the motives of immigrants. There were more pressing things to worry about than Morris's warped views on the country they'd battled and sacrificed everything to clash with.

He shifted his thoughts back to Vera and Harold. He envisioned her sad crumpled expression and the tears that would undoubtedly be trickling out. He had no idea what he was going to do next.

DETENTION

It took hours more until Harold finally came down from both the chemical high derived from the mouthful of meth, and the secondary one that was generated from tearing apart Tina. While his insides still stewed with bizarre emotions that he had no means of explaining, physically, he appeared normal enough to return to the single place that his mother believed brought a sense of normalcy to his life—school.

In spite of Vera's misconceptions, Harold had returned to the gloomy dungeon where he was hopelessly housed to receive his 'education' with his peers. He sat before Sister Doomus on a day that, in the easily entangled and overwhelmed minds of the students, had been about as good as they could have hoped for.

They all stared nervously at the wall clock, unable to tell time, but knowing the general area the hands needed to reach in order to go home. It wouldn't be much longer. Sister Doomus seemed to be finishing up her daily banter and Shelly, Benji, and Harold all remained obedient.

Suddenly, Sister Doomus's uncharacteristically calm demeanor shifted. "Harold! Stop looking at that clock! You should be focused on the message. You're never going to learn the Lord's way if your small mind remains elsewhere. Detention! And maybe after school's out, I'll find a way to hold your attention…"

A sinister calmness radiated from her as the words drifted out into the dingy air. A crooked grin smoothed out the wrinkles around her haggard lips as the bell finally rang.

"You stay here while I lead the others to the bus," Sister Doomus sneered at Harold.

***

After Sister Doomus dropped Shelly and Benji off at the short bus, she made her way back into the school's main office. Most of the personnel had already filed out or made their way back to the church or nunnery. Sister May, who didn't teach but attended to the office affairs, lifted up her purse as they caught each other's gaze.

"Is there anything I can help you with, Sister?" she asked innocently.

"The Harlow boy just doesn't seem to get it. He's going to need to stay after today," Sister Doomus replied.

"Again? My word, wasn't he kept after not even a month ago already?" Sister May asked.

"I'm afraid so. It's alright, sometimes the Lord just challenges us. There is no task too tall for me to attempt. He'll eventually get there, they all do. But, might I bother you to look up his mother's phone number for me before you leave?"

"Of course, would you like me to call for you?"

"That's alright, no sense in keeping the both of us here any longer," Sister Doomus replied.

"Well, that's very kind of you," Sister May replied, looking through a rolodex of student contact information. She let the deck rest upon locating the name Vera Harlow.

With the beige card pointed in Sister Doomus's direction, Sister May headed for the exit. Before she reached it, she turned back toward her peer.

"Should I leave the front door unlocked? I'll lock everything else, as usual, but can I assume the front door is where you'll instruct Mrs. Harlow to enter?"

"Yes, that's perfect. Thank you, and do have a good night, dear," Sister Doomus said with a grin.

Sister Doomus reached down between her legs and exhaled deeply. Over her habit, she rubbed just below the overgrown jungle of pubic hair that had stretched out her underwear over time. "Almost time," she whispered softly to herself.

She detracted her focus from the salivation-inducing subject that dominated her corrupt mind and quickly dialed out. After a few rings, the message machine hit.

"Hello, Mrs. Harlow, this is Sister Doomus from Saint Leo's. I'm afraid Harold has been acting inappropriately in class again… he's currently in detention for the time being. I suggest once you get the message, you come and discuss the next steps we need to take for your boy. The front door of the school will remain open after hours to accommodate you. Good day," she said, conjuring up the same sultry smirk.

***

When Sister Doomus returned to the bowels of the building, Harold still remained seated, exactly where he'd been when she left him. He sat at his desk, that blankness that was all he knew remained entrenched within his odd expression.

"I'm very disappointed in you, Harold. Sometimes I wonder if you'll ever grasp what's being offered to you. I'm here to show you the path, but I can't force you down it. I have a lesson for you," she explained, swishing her thighs against each other.

"After your lesson, we'll go upstairs and wait in the office for your mother, but first, you must learn. I pray for your soul. I pray that you will accept your education."

Sister Doomus stood in front of her desk and faced the chalkboard. She kept her back to Harold as she began to offer him her enlightenment.

"It isn't important where you find the Lord, just that you find him. He may be waiting to guide you from the most unexpected avenues. Places you would never imagine…"

Sister Doomus let her hand make its way under her habit and pulled at her underwear. Her crusty panties descended under her wrinkly kneecaps until she eventually worked them off altogether. They sat on the floor, simmering in her sticky juices of excitement.

"Even in the most forbidden and unconventional areas, you will find the Lord. Waiting there to guide you with his light. Waiting to show you the way," she explained, leaning over her desk.

In her bent-over pose, Sister Doomus began to elevate her habit until every inch of her wrinkled and crater-laden ass was exposed to Harold. As she spread her saggy legs wide, the disgusting divots rooted in her backside became further pronounced and her putrid pheromones percolated throughout the nasty room.

Harold's eyes remained fixated on the hag's vile bottom, but not just on her musty waterlogged flesh. He noticed something different. Something that he'd never seen around his own butt before.

Hanging from the center of Sister Doomus's greasy brown ring of release sat a symbol. The putrid puckered flesh was tight, and it held the metallic crucifix that Harold had noticed at the end of her abnormally large rosary beads days before, upright, as it should be.

For a moment, he wondered where the rest of the beads had gone. It was a mystery that he wasn't mentally equipped to solve. He just watched it waddle slightly from side to side as Sister Doomus's rectum began to pulsate.

"You must reach for the Lord, no matter where you are! You must follow him through the darkness, no matter what the circumstance! Stand up, Harold!" she yelled.

Harold found his footing, the thoughts inside his head grew more distorted with each moment he stared at her sphincter. He remembered seeing Tina's body—a woman uncovered for the first time. The uncanny feeling inside him, the feeling of her warmth against his body.

"Reach for the Lord, Harold! Pull him toward you! Let him take hold of you! Take the crucifix!" she screamed, lifting up a pair of number two pencils off of her desk and inserting them horizontally into her mouth.

As Harold's blubbery hand reached toward the attractive shining metal, Sister Doomus bit down. Carefully, he tugged them back in his direction, watching Sister Doomus's anus begin to gape, allowing the first profane strawberry-sized rosary bead to exit.

"YES! TAKE THE LORD! TAKE ALL OF HIM!" Sister Doomus wailed as she bit down harder on the number two pencils.

Harold's eyes turned black as he felt an otherworldly feeling grip him. Flashes of Tina's hacked-up pieces trickled into his warped mind. Flashes of the fat wicked man that guided him. It felt like he was still there. It felt like he now carried the man's morbid fibers, like he was inside him, driving Harold forward.

The next few beads gave way, along with an expulsion of lumpy fecal matter. The juicy mix of yellow and brown stained the rosary, caking to each bead that exited. It looked like something a dying dog might produce as his parting movement. It smelled like a combination of rancid meat, mothballs, and stagnant body odor. It was so potent, it could've been from the medieval era.

As Sister Doomus continued to relieve herself, her body shook with a perverse elation. The odorous rectal nectars drizzled down her thighs as she continued to cry, "TAKE THE LORD, HAROLD! TAKE HIM!"

Harold didn't know why he did it, it was pure instinct. Maybe the sick, fat man had put the thoughts in his head... if nothing else, he'd certainly planted the seed. Hurting her just felt right. It felt like something that should have happened a long time ago.

Sister Doomus didn't expect it when Harold jumped up on her back. The shit-smeared rosary slipped over her coif and veil, and then slid down to the many jiggly chins under her jaw before finally reaching her fragile neck.

She took a couple of steps backwards before falling face-first into a pasty pool of her own droppings. Harold remained fixed on her back, using his considerable weight to cut off the air in her windpipe with the sturdy metal rosary. He dug his beefy knees into her spine and pulled back with the rosary, twisting it as far as he could.

He cranked it to capacity as the rage took over. The bones in Sister Doomus's throat began to crack, different areas of the neck emitting different tones like he was tapping a xylophone.

As Harold began to feel the specialness inside him again, he eyed the sharpened number two pencil drenched in feces that laid on the ground beside Sister Doomus's fading face. He let his grip loosen on the rosary he was using to garrote the demonic nun with, and her face fell into the mustardy pool of shit beneath her.

Harold was so excited when his flabby fingers touched on the oily instrument. He knew what he needed to do, that much he'd been taught already. With one hand, he used the rosary to pull back Sister Doomus's head, while he readied the pencil in his other. He jammed the point of the lead down into her eye socket and pushed it as deep as his strength would allow.

The blood that squirted out of Sister Doomus's face excited him. It made Harold hard down there again to see it blasting its way out of her wicked body. He twisted and turned the slippery body of the writing utensil in and out, pushing in every direction imaginable. The optical puncture wound increased in size while the crimson cascaded and a translucent liquid drizzled down over the soupy human waste that sat under Sister Doomus's chin.

But irrespective of the horrific event and violence being viciously laid upon Sister Doomus, the nun had no reaction. Ironically, she was now inadvertently setting the example for the twisted lesson that she'd been trying to convey to Harold. She was now reaching for the Lord.

A MOMENT OF DREAD

I gripped the steering wheel in the car tight and firm—a combination of rage and anxiety was responsible for the roughhouse clutch. The rain pounded on the windshield like it was being launched from a Super Soaker. It always seemed to come on my darkest days.

Despite the problems I was dealing with, it had actually been a decent day. No conversations with Felix at work, and the rooms at The Lonely Bug weren't as trashed as they normally were. I got things done quickly enough to be home early in time for Harold's arrival.

But when I sat on the toilet and tried to relax for a moment, that's when the phone rang, of course. By the time I finished, it was too late. The voice message only confirmed that, despite how decent the day had gone, a wart would always find a way to corrupt the bigger picture.

As I drove the slick path toward Harold's school, I had my fears, but it was nothing too extreme. I knew that if he'd done something as terrible as he'd done at The Lonely Bug, it wouldn't be a nun that was calling me, it would be the police. Still, the way I felt wasn't any kind of way to feel.

I had higher hopes after Sunday. Hopes that would allow things to go back to normal again. Normal for us anyway. Normal in the way that there was no violence. I had no choice in the matter but to leave Harold tied to the bed for the remainder of the Saturday when he'd ingested the meth. He looked like a sick rabid animal at first. Frothing and screeching wildly. He'd been calm until I coaxed him into a restrained state. He didn't like that, but it had to be that way.

On Sunday morning, he was like a different person. He'd returned to the bizarre boy that I'd come to love. The one I prayed would blossom out of the chaos he'd been conceived amid. Quiet, naïve, and docile, Harold no longer jerked the ropes he was bound by. The headboard no longer smacked against the wall behind it. The scowl that had smothered him during his stupor had lifted; the hatred had faded, or at least been halted.

That Sunday consisted of Harold watching cartoons and me dissecting the events of the prior day. I still wondered if Harold was going to stay grounded, but as he showed no signs of returning to the uncontrollable state he'd launched into, my mind became consumed with larger issues. Issues that needed to be addressed immediately.

What was I going to do with Tina's corpse? Was Daniel ever coming back? The good thing was, if he did, at least he wasn't capable of venturing downstairs and discovering the innocent girl's mutilated remains.

As I pulled into the empty parking lot behind the school, I knew whatever had caused Harold's detention couldn't have been that bad. Yet, somehow, an instinctual feeling of profound trepidation still lingered inside me. My maternal dismay hadn't let me down before, something told me that it wouldn't today either…

SON OF THE SLOB

I rushed in through the front door, trying to get out of the downpour that dominated the atmosphere. Just as Sister Doomus had explained, it remained open. The main office was empty and the halls were dark. There was a silence that sent chills running throughout my body.

I hadn't ventured far into the school's interior before. My prior interactions were in the main office area, so I didn't know what to think when I found it empty. I had no choice but to venture into the classrooms.

"Hello?" I called out.

I expected a response but got nothing. There were two primary floors that I was aware of, but I'd never actually set foot in Harold's classroom before. Without a route in mind, I walked up to each of the doors on the first floor and peered in through the vertical panes of wiry glass. The angle allowed me to see each of the teacher's desks and also a few rows of the student seating.

Each one offered the same empty results, and each knob I attempted to turn was locked. I couldn't imagine that the students who were special education would be on the upper floor, but that was the only other place I could think of to check next.

As I ascended the old marbled staircase, my heart pounded in my chest. "Hello, Sister Doomus?!" I yelled a little louder this time. "It's Vera Harlow, are you up here with Harold?" I continued fruitlessly.

It didn't take me long to perform the same exercise on the upper floor that I had done below. But surprisingly, it yielded the same results. As I descended the steps and arrived back on the first floor, my confusion only grew.

My eyes then arrived on the one place that remained an option. An unlikely option, but an option nonetheless. *Who would hold class in a basement?* I thought.

The idea made me shudder as I took my first step downward. When I reached the bottom of the steps, a dusty and chipped door stood before me. I didn't want to open it—not only did the ominous ascetics disturb me but also the lingering feeling of queasiness that had found a home in my stomach. But it wasn't as if I could just turn around.

The door was unlocked, and as I pulled it closer toward me, I heard a faint knocking noise that sounded like marbles crashing together. When the scene was presented to me, I nearly lost the ability to stand. My knees weakened and I used the door handle to hold myself up as I looked on at the mayhem in total revulsion.

Sister Doomus laid face-down in a motionless heap. Her clothing baring her naked shit-caked behind, and her face buried in a messy puddle of runny feces and blood. A pencil embedded in her eyeball protruded outward and a mixture of blood and orbital fluid dripped down her excrement-drenched face. The ghoulish expression left me speechless as her fluids raced down the wrinkles in her leathery skin.

She certainly wasn't making the noise. She was no longer capable of such a feat. Hell had found my sights again as my eyes drifted upward to the source. Harold sat cross-legged on her back, holding a set of uncharacteristically massive rosary beads. I could clearly see that they were covered in Sister Doomus's bodily waste. Well, some of them were…

The noise was the sound of the colossal black beads clacking against Harold's decaying choppers. He was filled with joy as he suckled the fecal matter off each of the individual beads. Once he cleaned one, he moved onto the next. The gross Tuscany waste covered his plump fingers and ran down his stubbly chin.

"Harold… what have you… what have you done?" I said, unable to hide my disbelief.

He didn't say a word to me, he just continued to clean the religious jewelry like a cat does its own asshole.

"Why?! Why did you do this, Harold?!" I yelled.

My words had little to no impact on him. He certainly wasn't ready to share, so I could only imagine. The scene was so fucking weird in appearance, that if Columbo walked in, it would've left him puzzled. There was no solving this thing and wrapping it up at the end of the episode.

Panic took hold of me as I staggered into the room. I was losing my footing; my legs were giving out. I stumbled behind what I could only assume was Sister Doomus's desk. I was able to land in the seat and keep my bearings.

"Stay awake, stay awake," I whispered.

I looked around the classroom and took in the surroundings. Something was clearly off. The drippy pipes and generally filthy environment weren't suitable conditions to teach children in. The place looked more like a dungeon than a classroom. It looked… more like our house…

Why are they down here in such conditions? I wondered.

As the thunder boomed outside of the building, my eye caught a glimmer of something shiny to my right. A keyring was lodged into Sister Doomus's desk. I didn't know what to do next, but something told me to look in the drawer.

My fingers curled around the iron handle and I shifted the wooden box toward me. Inside didn't give me the entire answer, but it gave me an idea. A dark and sickening idea of the level of depravity that Harold and the other children were being subjected to.

The Polaroid camera sat in the back of the drawer, and the front was littered with a buffet of disgusting images. In each of the dozen or so white sheets of photography, I found my son. He was naked and made to pose in a variety of lewd and compromising positions. In some pictures, he had various religious objects inserted into his mouth. In others, they chose to occupy his rectal region. Each photo that I revealed was more enraging than the prior.

The sick bitch was torturing him! In the one place that I'd believed he was starting to show promise, they were fucking him up worse than anywhere else. Suddenly, it all made sense—his outlandish behavior, anti-social nature, and difficulty developing. Was Saint Leo's the root cause behind Harold's lack of evolution?

This fucking place wasn't here to help. They were here under a guise. To pluck the downtrodden and damaged and have their perverse way with them. A picture is worth a thousand words, and I had nearly a dozen of them that were all telling me the dead bitch on the floor was an imposter. An imposter that deserved every bit of Harold's dark side.

As horrifying as my son's actions over the past few days have been, there's no way I could blame him for them. The situations he'd found himself in, through no fault of his own, were more than nefarious. In fact, many of them reminded me of my own.

The helplessness he must have felt being here. I know what it feels like to be trapped. I know what it feels like to have no one. There is no worse feeling than the harrowing isolation that he's been forced to endure for God knows how long now.

But how does it end? Where can I go from here? Where can we go from here? The questions echoed in my overwhelmed skull as I took hold of the scattered Polaroids and gathered them up. I slipped them into my pants and looked around that poor excuse for a classroom again.

How do I get us out of this?

I set my gaze upon the pair of restrooms at the far end of the space. I opened the boy's room and found a small closet inside. Upon entry, I noticed a mop bucket and collection of cleaning supplies. I exhaled a big huff of stress and tried to push the totality of the spiraling events of the past few days out of my head.

My arms were shaking uncontrollably. *I can't lose it now, Harold needs me. He doesn't have anyone else who can understand what he's been through. How unfair can the hand you're dealt in life be? I need to be strong for him.*

It was time to go to work.

THE PILE GROWS

Cleaning up the mess took me hours to complete. Bagging and dragging Sister Doomus's hefty body up a flight of basement steps, and waiting for the right moment to work her into the car, was even more strenuous. The rain didn't help matters much.

Conveniently, the school was relatively secluded, and there wasn't any other housing outside of the nunnery that was all the way on the other side of the school. With traffic on the road being non-existent, I was able to load her into the back of my car, just as I had done with Tina.

As I placed Sister Doomus beside the bags in the basement that contained Tina's remains, I felt a slight sense of relief. Nothing was solved, but at least I was done for the moment. At least Harold and I were both safe, and I could begin to consider what the next steps were going to be.

First things first, I needed to get rid of them. I needed to find out the best place or means to dispose of them both. I wanted to give Tina the benefit of the doubt, but the more I thought about the situation and the more I saw the veil pulled back on the rest of the 'good people' of the world, the less credibility my heart wanted to lend. I could feel it growing colder and less considerate by the second.

People were shit, even the ones that you thought you could count on just disappeared after being by your side for decades. While I didn't want to think about him in that light, I was beginning to include Daniel in that conversation. Maybe not entirely, but I was still pained by his absence, although I had little time to truly think about it as of late.

The notion caused my mind to shift back to the current horror that surrounded me. Sister Doomus was dead, which meant she wouldn't be teaching class tomorrow. The church would immediately suspect something was amiss, certainly tomorrow, maybe even tonight.

I couldn't let Harold go back to that school, not after what they'd done to him. But pulling him out would undoubtedly create suspicion in the mind of whoever examined the details surrounding her 'disappearance.' Saying Harold was sick tomorrow was probably the most reasonable option, there wasn't much else I could do.

I was beginning to feel like my head was about to explode. The pressure was crushing down on me like my temples were trapped between a vice grip. The thoughts were all of darkness and came in abundance.

I have no one to talk to anymore, except for Harold, but he can't properly hold a conversation. I need to sort some things out in my head before I unravel.

Then, suddenly, I remembered Dr. Plankton... maybe he'd be willing to see me on short notice. I couldn't share everything that was going on with him, all that I'd been through, but maybe he could assist in some of the less controversial and incriminating aspects. He wasn't the best doctor, but he'd always found a way to be helpful in the past.

I left the basement and locked the door. Then I headed to the kitchen and opened up a can of Dinty Moore beef stew. I dumped the lumpy contents of the can into a bowl and set it to microwave for a few minutes.

Once it was finished, I took the steaming stew over to Harold's room and opened the door. He seemed tired, laying on his bed for once instead of chasing after the rats. I set the bowl at the side of his bed and whispered, "Mommy has to go out for a little, Harold. Please, stay in your room. You need to eat and rest now, okay?" I asked, not expecting an answer.

I left the hearty stew on his bed and gave him a brief hug. When we pulled apart, I stepped back toward the exit and then closed his door. I looked at the new lock that I'd installed on the door's exterior. It was sturdy, which was good—it needed to be.

I had purchased it after work, his first incident of extreme violence left me with many questions. Trust continued to be an issue in my mind. While I still loved Harold and believed in him, there was a part of me that remained cautious and uncertain. A part of me that felt uncomfortable with him roaming freely of his own warped will. A part of me that continued to see his depraved father in his eyes.

Would he overcome or become him? There was no way to be certain. I had debated installing the lock, but with the disturbing imagery of the past few days still simmering in my brain, it didn't really seem like a choice anymore. It was a completely rational precaution. Which is why I installed it even before I dragged Sister Doomus's lifeless corpse into the basement.

I locked Harold inside his room before making my way back to the kitchen. The vile garbage and scurry of the overfed roaches made my skin crawl. The flies had become a problem as of late too. They had always been there, but never in such numbers. The weather was getting a bit warmer, maybe that was the reason.

The mild heat only amplified the already potent scents that smothered us on a daily basis. I looked down at a partially ripped garbage bag near my knees. The rotten food was moving—the maggots twitched with delight, enjoying their foul, never-ending meal.

Would this place ever be different? Could we ever go back to the way things were? Or were we just destined to be disgusting human beings? When I died (of natural causes, or otherwise…), would the police and firemen all burst in through the doors and eventually discover that these rats and maggots had accounted for my spoiled remains? Would this house literally consume me?

I felt dizzy just pondering the future. Those were questions that I shouldn't even be thinking about, yet they were realistic and, even scarier, probable.

"What a bizarre life I've led," I whispered to myself.

I pushed the thoughts out of my brain and refocused. There weren't many positives I had to draw from, and there weren't many shoulders to cry on. I approached the phone hanging on the side of the wall and lifted it up to my ear. Underneath where the phone sat, there was a tiny list of emergency and frequently used numbers taped to the base. Dr. Plankton's number was at the top of the list.

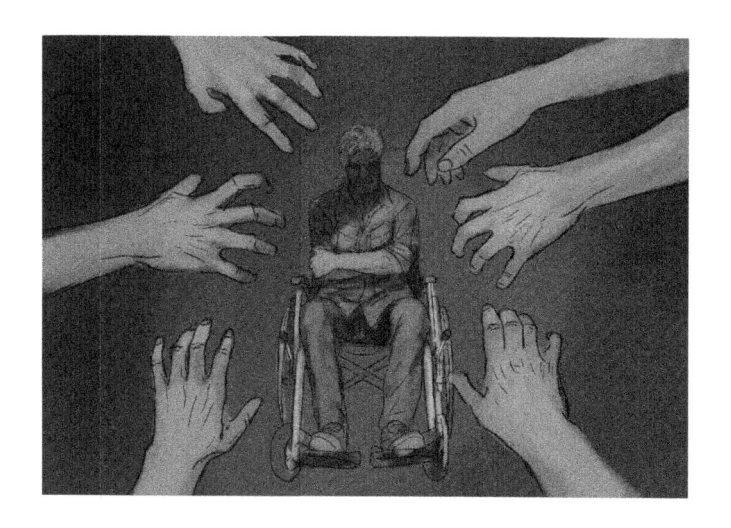

THE GUILT OF A GUARDIAN

Daniel stared at the flicker of the television mindlessly. The old snowy reruns that graced the screen did little to distract him. His life was in shambles, and he sat at a dark crossroads pondering potential outcomes.

The prior evening's ghastly nightmare hadn't made him feel better about his decision to leave Vera and Harold. If anything, it made him feel self-centered. It took recalling the accidental deed that he'd committed during wartimes to see the situation from a different perspective.

Daniel had tried to erase the act from his mind, first with the bottle, then through therapy, and finally, with Vera. It became a far and distant memory that he'd locked away under the layers of self-medication and post-alcoholism, with the warm love that Vera had granted him. He'd successfully avoided triggering it… until he left.

Now it had once again resurfaced, but he felt like there was a reason for it. Daniel had been thinking about the dream for the better part of the day, and now realized how selfish he was. He'd taken someone else's life and the life of their unborn, the least he could've done was give a chance to someone that was born without one.

In Daniel's mind, no matter how cryptic and dark the situation at home was, it wasn't worse than the one that unfolded on the battlefield in Vietnam.

He'd been given an incredible and strong woman in Vera who'd suffered unimaginable agony. She was in a horrible position due to no fault of her own, and he'd left her. He'd left her alone to flounder in uncertainty with an unstable boy. It was the kind of decision that might have pushed her over the edge. The sort of permanent pressure that he'd left Vera with was the variety that might help spawn a nervous breakdown.

Was that who he was? A man that took life and turned his back when he had the chance to help foster it? He was on the wrong track for a while, it took Vera to snatch him from the clutches of death and despair. He could've helped to do the same for her, but instead, he was slumped over on Morris's sofa, feeling bad for himself again.

Daniel knew exactly what he needed to do now. He needed to make amends for the innocent lives he'd drawn a conclusion upon. He needed to go back to Vera and Harold and grind it out. Change his attitude. Find a way to help make things better instead of making them worse.

Daniel heard the toilet in the bathroom flush, and a moment later, Morris appeared, still buckling his belt.

"You might wanna stay clear of the facilities for a while," Morris said, pointing into the bathroom, "I'm not sure what's come over me," he warned.

Daniel smiled, "Those burgers seemed a little off. I hope I'm not next."

"Yeah, Burger Billy's ain't exactly how we remembered it. New management can fuck a place up entirely."

"Whoever took that place over should be shot. How hard can it be? The place was perfect already."

"Exactly, that spot was a goddamn goldmine when we were kids! But now it looks more like a ghost town. I can't believe they fell off like that, it's a fuckin' tragedy," Morris said with depression caressing his tone.

"Yeah, the secret sauce isn't really a secret anymore. That was just Thousand-Island dressing…" Daniel concurred.

"Fuckin' bullshit," Morris replied, sitting down in the chair a short distance away from the couch. Daniel was laying quietly with a smile on his face, but Morris could see he wasn't happy. His eyes told a different story.

"So, what's on your mind?" Morris asked.

"Huh?" Daniel tried to play it off. He wasn't sure if he wanted to talk about it at the moment.

"You been sitting there all day just thinking. You act like you're watching the shows, but you damn well know you aren't. Talk to me, don't bullshit me."

They hadn't seen each other in years, but the man still knew him about as good as anyone. Daniel exhaled and turned to meet his gaze.

"I think I need to go back…" he confessed.

"Okay… I figured you eventually would… but you mean now?" Morris asked.

"I can wait until tomorrow. I don't wanna put you out, plus I still have a few things in my head to sort out. I'm sorry, man, I know this is all very random… is that cool?"

"Danny boy, I think you're doing the right thing. Your family needs you. You fought this long to get where you are, there's a light at the end of this for you. I'd give anything to have what you have still. I know you'll make it work," Morris said with a melancholic smile.

A new commitment manifested in Daniel's pupils. The period of reflection had lit a fire inside him. He nodded at Morris and said, "I'm sure as hell gonna try."

TELL ME YOUR WOES

Dr. Plankton was dressed as snooty as normal, but the typical look of boredom and mild annoyance that constantly flowed down his face had been replaced with pity. He didn't normally see clients on such short notice or at such a late hour, but when he heard me break down on the phone and explain that Daniel had left, the ice casing around his heart must have started to defrost.

I couldn't stop rocking my leg up and down as I watched him jot down a few things into his trusty pad. He knew I was in a bad way and sacrificed his own (probably boring) evening to accommodate me.

"Did he say if he was coming back? Maybe he just needed a little space, sometimes that happens with people. They go through too much and it just becomes too crushing to deal with reality," Dr. Plankton offered.

"He didn't say anything," I replied.

"Okay, so I'm assuming you don't know where he is and haven't heard from him since?"

"That's right." I wiped a tear streak away from my cheek. "I just don't know if… if I can do it without him. It's too much, I just wake up sometimes and feel like I can't breathe, it's like I'm suffocating. Maybe it would be better if I was dead. If this sick joke was all finally over. There's not a day it doesn't cross my mind. I've yearned for that kind of relief since I can remember."

"You may not think so, but trust me when I say this, Vera, the world is a much better place with people like you."

"But maybe I want to be selfish for once," I replied.

He didn't entertain the thought of my demise any further, instead, he moved on to discussing the other difficulties that I had mentioned. "Regarding the issues with breathing, it sounds like a panic attack. It's something that affects many people, stress can have a miraculous impact on the human physique. If those incidents continue, we might be able to get you a prescription to help. How is Harold taking all of this? Has Daniel's absence had an impact? Has he been alright?"

More tears pushed from my sockets before I could even begin to try and tackle that question. "He's the same as he always is—oblivious," I lied. "I just don't even know what to do, it's all one giant mess!" I slammed my fist down on his desk in front of me.

"Vera, please, I need you to relax, I'm here to help you, okay? I know this can't be easy, I know that it feels like every factor is against you, but you've beaten those odds before, remember?" Dr. Plankton asked with a subtle strain of discomfort attached to his tone.

"This isn't some fight for life against a single individual, it's much more complicated than all that! Miracles don't just grow on fucking trees!" I couldn't help but think about the bodies in my basement. I wanted to explain more, but I knew I couldn't.

"If anyone can do it, it's you. You're an inspirational human being. I know that you can do it, I've seen you do it for years now," Dr. Plankton reassured me.

"But I've never done it alone... I've never done it alone..."

"Maybe not, but that doesn't mean you can't."

His words helped, even though it was only just a bit, they still were something. They were the only words that I was able to seek for guidance, I may not have had the ability to show it outwardly, but I appreciated his general positivity and encouragement.

"I-I'm sorry, I don't know what's come over me. Sometimes I just get so mad. Sometimes I just see red. I mean, how bad can life fucking get?" I felt fear as a result of the wicked thoughts and imagery that was saturating my skull. I didn't feel like myself anymore. I felt completely broken.

"You mustn't let your anger control you. No matter how bad things get, trust me when I say, they can always get worse."

"Can they?"

"Yes, they can."

"Tell me, how does it get worse? Because they certainly aren't getting any better! So, tell me, Doctor, how fucking bad does it get for me?!" I was screaming now, but it actually felt good in a strange way. Although, I could tell from Dr. Plankton's slack-jawed expression it was making him highly uncomfortable.

"Right now, Daniel could still come back. It's only been a few days, right? Who's to say that he isn't just reflecting? Who's to say that he isn't trying to catch his breath. I would imagine that if you're suffocating, he's probably in a similar predicament, wouldn't you?"

"I suppose..."

"But if he returns, and you're acting like this, if you're enraged and out of control, how do you think he'll feel?"

"Not good."

"Right. Do you think that he'll stay with you again if you're acting like this? Or do you think it's more probable that he'll head right back the way that he came?"

"He would probably leave again."

I watched Dr. Plankton scribble down many more notes in his pad. I don't think I'd ever seen him write so excitedly. Maybe it was the overall awkwardness and uncertainty of our conversation. Maybe it was my increasingly fragile state. Regardless, he was finding many noteworthy details in our emotional exchange.

"So, what we can do is begin taking steps toward creating an atmosphere and environment that would be more appealing to Daniel. Finding ways to move forward and grow in his absence. How does that sound to you?"

"What if he doesn't come back?"

"You're jumping ahead. Did he say he wasn't coming back, or leave you a message? Is there something you haven't told me?"

What a fucking loaded question that was. I would need to keep it in the context of Daniel and just answer as best I could. That was all I could offer him.

"No, like I said, he didn't say anything to me. I just came home one evening and he was gone. Cold turkey."

"So, why are you so sure that he's not going to come home? In my experience, these situations tend to be largely temporary."

"After I brought Daniel here to talk for a session, things just continued to get worse. Our communication was already bad, but it became non-existent. He just shut down. He didn't give me any reason to think he's coming back. I mean, realistically, what do I have to offer? Problems? A mentally retarded child from a fucking murderer? A destroyed body, mind, and soul? The rotten stench of deep depression? I'm fucking worthless!" I screamed.

I don't know why I rose to my feet. I was just so angry that I couldn't even sit anymore. I was grinding my teeth and clenching my fists. What the hell was wrong with me?

"Vera, please, just sit down and try to relax, we can figure this out together, okay? We can still figure it out, I promise you," Dr. Plankton pleaded.

I slapped the writing utensil receptacle at the edge of his desk clear across the room. It smashed into a glass vase that held a handful of wilting flowers.

"What don't you fucking get! There's nothing to figure out anymore! It's over! It's done! I'm gone! There's no coming back again!"

I tossed my chair sideways. The anger inside me was changing me. I didn't know who I was anymore. This wasn't me; I was now the imprint of the damages bestowed upon me. It was a dangerous feeling.

I took one last look at Dr. Plankton and the utter shock that drenched his face. For the first time ever, he was speechless. I didn't hear a word leave his lips as I ran out of his office. I needed to leave before my emotions escalated past the line that they'd already crossed.

LOCKED AWAY

Every time I stepped into Room 13, it gave me chills. It was a space of unimaginable horror and I had no doubt that each time I entered, I would feel the same way. I never wanted to clean up the remnants of a murder scene. I never wanted to see Harold carrying on with his father's twisted traditions. I never wanted to cut up a body. But it had all happened in that room and God knew what else. If the walls could talk, they probably wouldn't. They'd probably just scream.

Upon entry, I was overcome with a mixture of feelings. On one hand, I was horrified at the thought of reliving the trauma, and on the other, I was happy that it was the last room I had to clean before I left for the day.

I kept thinking about poor Harold and the lock I'd installed outside of his door. I still couldn't trust him to be left to his own devices. I had no other option but to lock him away for the time being. He wasn't safe to roam the house, but it also wasn't safe to bring him back to The Lonely Bug based on the last incident.

I certainly couldn't send him back to the school with those demons. I didn't believe it was just Sister Doomus, most likely, she was just a part of the problem. Even if she was the entire problem, I couldn't risk sending Harold any further down the rabbit hole at this point. I'd decided to go with the lone temporary solution that I concocted the prior evening—calling in sick for him and keeping him at home.

At least he would be safe. At least he wouldn't be getting defiled by that sick woman or anyone else. I wanted to pray for better days but wasn't sure anything would come of it. The other people, like Sister Doomus, who were entranced in prayer, weren't doing much better.

The thought of her rotting in my basement entertained me momentarily as I began to gather the empty beer cans and fast-food wrappers from the table and nightstands. *You got what you damn well deserved,* I thought.

It was easy enough for me to understand, but convincing a jury would be far more difficult. I had the pictures, but I didn't call the police. Did molestation justify murder? In my mind, the answer was obvious, but as evidenced by the events of recent weeks, no one else was a safe bet.

If you added the Tina situation into the equation, that makes it far more difficult. How could I explain it all to the authorities? If I had called them when I found Sister Doomus's defiled corpse, a detailed investigation was sure to follow. Most likely a thorough search of the house. The conditions alone could've probably landed me in prison.

It was just like before, I had to clean it up. I had to make it go away. No bodies, no charges. That was what I was thinking in my head as I stripped down the bedding and dropped it into the laundry bag.

Marlboro Bridge was just a short drive away from the house. It was seldom trafficked, so maybe one night I could load both of them into my car with a couple of weights and just send them off the side. It didn't sound that difficult when I considered it. It didn't seem like it would take more than a few hours to be rid of them.

The water was deep enough that they would most likely never be found. I recalled a news story on the television from a few years prior. The news anchor spoke soberly about some poor guy who committed suicide there. A car passing by just saw him stand up on the rail and slowly let himself drift backwards. By the time the witness got out of the car, it was already too late. To this day, his body still hasn't been found.

Out of all the ideas that had been fighting for attention inside my head, this one gave me some hope. *I'll go late at night when there's almost no traffic. There's definitely some rope in the house... what about the weights? I don't think we have anything that would suffice... I'll have to check, maybe there is something in the basement that I can use? If not, no biggie, I can always stop at the store if I need to.*

I felt just a little bit disgusted with myself for deriving excitement from such a morbid thought. But it was just the nature of who I was in the moment. I was a woman trying to protect my only son from being imprisoned under unjustifiable circumstances.

The most open mind wouldn't be able to swallow the whopper that I was going to hit them with. Even when I played it over in my head, I couldn't help but feel like the tale sounded fantastical. Something you might read in a horror book or low-budget film.

Finally, I had a plan. But I was going to need to execute it quickly before anyone starts asking quest—

There was a knock that came from the ajar door behind me. I turned to be greeted by one familiar face and one stranger. Detective Wells and his draping navy blue overcoat blended into the overcast of clouds behind him seamlessly. A black man stood to his right dressed similarly. He was wearing wide shades unnecessarily and puffing on a long cigarette. Their expressions mirrored each other—they were both dead serious.

"Vera, it's good to see you again," Detective Wells said with a certain degree of smugness.

"D-Detective Wells, was it?" The detective and his friend had caught me completely off guard and it showed. My tone wreaked of a person who had something to hide.

"That's right. Everything okay? You seem a bit… I don't know, nervous?"

"It's just this room, it gives me the creeps still," I wasn't lying, but it was for different reasons than he was aware of.

"That's funny, last time it didn't really seem that way. Anyhow, you're probably wondering why myself and my colleague, Detective Bates, are here, right?"

He positioned the question to me in a way that would seem to paint me with some kind of inside knowledge of whatever crime he might have arrived to discuss. I played stupid and just nodded my head slowly. There wasn't much else I could do.

"Well, it's a small world I suppose. And I'm well aware of that fact, and I know that *because* it's a small world, it's particularly important to be *real* good with names. As you're already aware, I work homicide. Detective Bates here works missing persons. I just happened to overhear that on his latest case, the last person in contact with the missing… was you. So, as I said, small world."

"Oh my God, really? Who is it? I'll help with the case however I'm able to," I moused in response.

I tried to sound as natural and shocked to hear the news as I could. Hopefully, I didn't sound *too* shocked. I never fancied myself an actress, and I never felt comfortable lying. It was something that I'd had very little practice at. I'm sure that, in their eyes, I was doing a shitty job, but I just needed to do my best. It was difficult asking questions that I already knew the answers to. I just hoped that my words and reactions sounded authentic enough to avoid being arrested.

"You have a son, Harold Harlow, is that correct?" Detective Bates interjected, allowing a thick gray cloud of nicotine to exit his face. His aura was scary to me, like a fire-breathing dragon that was getting ready to eat me up. Detective Bates looked the opposite of me—fearless.

"Yes, that's correct."

"And does Harold have a teacher by the name of Sister Deloris Doomus?" he continued.

"Yes, oh God, is she the one who's gone missing now?"

"I'm afraid so. She never returned to the…" he looked over to Detective Wells. "What's the place again?"

"The nunnery," Detective Wells offered.

"The nunnery, she never returned home last night, Mrs. Harlow. After her meeting with you, she just disappeared, no one has seen or heard from her since," Detective Bates said, taking another massive drag of his cigarette.

"That's terrible, I mean, but it hasn't been *that* long though, has it? Don't police typically wait twenty-four hours or something? I know I've stayed with friends a few times here and there, out of the blue, could it be something like that possibly?" What the hell was I rambling on about? I would have been better off keeping my mouth shut, but I was nervously chattering away.

"Well, this is a little different," Detective Wells said.

"Oh, really?" I asked.

"Really," Detective Wells replied.

"How so? If you don't mind me asking, that is…"

"Sister Doomus is a sixty-eight-year-old woman who hasn't missed a day of school in over a decade, furthermore, she's never stayed anywhere outside of that…" Detective Bates looked over at Detective Wells for a moment.

"Nunnery," Detective Wells offered once again.

"That nunnery since she arrived in 1942. That's right, the roaring forties. I'd say those factors warrant an extenuating circumstance, wouldn't you?" Detective Bates asked.

"Of course, I was just, you know… you see television shows and whatnot, I didn't mean to—"

"Cut the shit, Vera, okay?" Detective Wells commanded.

I nodded my head again and ceased my speech.

"We didn't come here so you could ask us twenty fucking questions, alright? You should know from your TV shows that the first forty-eight hours in a missing person's investigation are the most important. So, what do you say we get down to it?" I could see that Detective Wells was a little sore at me, but I wasn't sure if he was truly suspicious yet. But I knew one thing, if I was in his position, I would be suspicious to the moon and back.

"I understand, I just... I just want to help is all," I replied.

"Great, you've got a tremendous opportunity, being that you were the last person to contact her. If you really help out then start by explaining exactly what happened during that meeting at the school? Tell us everything that happened last night," Detective Wells commanded.

"Nothing really, as you know, sh-she kept him, Harold, I mean, after class yesterday for detention. My son has some learning disabilities, sometimes it can be difficult for him to stay focused in the classroom. I suspect that's what it was about," I replied. As soon as the words left my mouth, I knew I'd fucked up. I couldn't believe I'd answered in that manner. My only hope is that they weren't smart enough to pick up on it. But of course, I had no such luck.

"Suspect? What do you mean suspect? She didn't tell you the reason why she held Harold after class?" Detective Bates chimed in.

"No, th-that's not what I meant... she said that he was talking to another classmate during a lesson. I just... I assume it was his short attention span that was the root of the issue. That's all I meant by it. Sorry for the confusion." I thought the recovery was pretty damn good. I didn't like lying, but at least I was getting better at it. I was going to need to if I wanted to swerve them.

Still, regardless of my salvaging explanation, I was not acting normal by any means. Detective Wells had seen me feeling confident, speaking like I had nothing to hide. I knew his intuition smelled something fishy. I was on the ropes, and if I wasn't careful with my next words, the detectives could deliver the knockout blow to me. I needed to focus. I needed to get through this conversation and get

SON OF THE SLOB

the fuck over to Marlboro Bridge as fast as possible.

"Did you ever have any issues with Sister Doomus before this? Arguments, disagreements? Anything at all helps, and trust me, we're going to find out, regardless," Detective Bates asked, lowering his shades slightly and looking directly into my eyes.

"Certainly, no arguments or disagreements. Believe it or not, school was the one place that Harold was making quite a bit of progress. Saint Leo's has a great program that offers free tuition to a few mentally disabled students each year. I was fortunate enough to be selected into the program, there was no way I was going to be able to pay for an education like that myself. I'm incredibly grateful for all they've done for us. So, no, there are no gripes for me to speak of, Saint Leo's has gone above and beyond for us."

"Where were you in the school when you discussed these issues with your boy, Mrs. Harlow? It's important we know any areas that you might've ventured to," Detective Bates explained.

"I met them in the main office. We talked there for a few minutes in the office first, and then in the hallway before we left. We didn't go anywhere else while I was there."

I had thought ahead and thoroughly wiped down all the areas I'd remembered touching inside the school. I went back and cleaned every single doorknob I tugged on. My fingerprints shouldn't be an issue, they weren't on file with the police, and they wouldn't be found anywhere else.

I wanted to keep them out of the basement where the murder had occurred. Whatever I could say to keep the two of them away from the murder scene, I would. Because of the deplorable conditions in what I knew to be Harold's classroom, I doubt the church would ever pony up to the fact that they were teaching students in such a filthy and unsanitary space.

I didn't imagine that they would find any kind of obvious evidence, or my fingerprints anywhere outside of the office. If there was one thing in my fucked-up life that I could bank on, it was my ability to clean up.

Detective Bates jotted down a few notes as I finished my answers. I couldn't tell what he was thinking, the man was incredibly hard to read.

"Okay," Detective Bates replied.

"So, how did it end?" Detective Wells asked.

"End?" I wasn't quite understanding, maybe because there were so many other fearful thoughts racing around my skull. Again, I hoped I seemed cooperative enough.

"I mean, after you discussed Harold's behavioral issues, then what happened?" Detective Wells inquired.

"She told me to have Harold say four Hail Mary's and one Our Father when we got home. Those are prayers... and then she asked that I try to explain to him that disrupting the class not only impacts him, but it impacts the other students that are trying to learn." I was making it up, but it really sounded like it could've happened. I felt the lie seemed credible for the first time during our exchange, mainly because I leveraged what Sister Doomus had said to me from the first detention she'd given Harold some time ago. The realism assisted in the story's authenticity.

"And then what?" Detective Bates prodded.

"And then we just left. Got in the car and drove home. It really wasn't that big of an issue. I think Sister Doomus just wanted to nip it before it escalated any further. I'm sure you know nuns can be rather strict," I said.

They both looked at me with a deadpan stare, letting the tension linger. Letting me simmer in it for a while. Knowing the level of discomfort I was feeling. They wanted me to sweat, they wanted to see if I would crack. They didn't have a fucking clue what real pressure was. They couldn't jog a crosswalk in my shoes.

Detective Bates slid his glasses up from the mid-point of his nose and let them cover both of his eyes again. He turned to Detective Wells and said, "I wouldn't know, I never went to Catholic school."

"Me neither," Detective Wells said. "But that's always

what I hear."

"She's a great woman, just a little on the tough side is all," I said, forcing a smile.

"Okay then. Anything else you'd like to add, Mrs. Harlow?" Detective Bates asked.

"No, it was a very transactional exchange. I'm afraid there's really nothing else to say. Except that I hope you find her, of course…"

Detective Bates reached into his coat pocket and removed a card. He handed it to me and said, "Don't travel anywhere far away for a few days. We may need to follow up with you… and if you can think of anything, and I mean anything else, you call me."

"Okay," I replied, taking the business card from him.

"We'll be in touch," Detective Wells said, tipping his hat and offering his smartass smirk again.

Through the cracked blinds of the motel window, I watched the two of them get into their vehicle and exit the dreary parking lot. I was now shaking wildly. My nerves were in overdrive. The adrenaline from the situation was blasting through my system.

Were they onto me? There was no way I could be sure either way. But there was one thing I was sure of—I needed to get rid of the fucking bodies in my basement.

HOMECOMING

Daniel closed the door behind him and locked it. He was all nerves but it still felt good to be back. In the pits of his soul, he knew it was where he was supposed to be. It was his destiny. He had finally arrived with a motive... no matter how bad things got, there was always a way to navigate them and make them work. He'd come full circle and wholly felt like he understood his purpose. It was time to balance out the forgotten weight on his spirit. It was time to do his part.

Morris seemed to be going through his own issues, part of Daniel felt bad that he couldn't be there more for his brother. He looked at the crumpled picture of the two of them in his hand. Even in the green inferno, while in the grips of a horrific war, they looked so full of life and vigor; a far cry from their current situations. Maybe it wouldn't be the last time they talked. Maybe he could still help him get past his demons. In a perfect world, that's how he envisioned things to play out. There would be a happy ending for not just him, but for everyone.

He felt like it was more than just a possibility, but it had to be a secondary priority considering the direction Daniel was headed. There was a lot to overcome before that could even be feasible. First things first.

The task ahead wasn't going to be easy, but regardless of how treacherous the situation grew, he wasn't going to give up this time. Just knowing that there was no hesitation in his heart would help him cope through the difficult times that undoubtedly laid ahead. It would help him climb to a level of resilience that he'd never elevated to before.

Daniel slipped the picture into his pocket and felt his pulse start to fluster. The silence was always uncomfortable in his mind. He couldn't hear any noise in the house, it was like even the rats and roaches were flabbergasted by his return. He peeked down at his watch and then over to the kitchen area that was still in shambles.

Vera wouldn't be home from work for a little while longer and Harold usually got dropped off about an hour or so before she arrived. It wasn't odd that no one was roaming about, he just had the jitters.

Daniel couldn't wait to see her again; it had only been a couple of days but it felt like a lifetime. The last stretch that they'd been separated for any amount of time was when Vera had been held captive at the farm. He remembered how difficult that period was for him. To be away from her, to be worried about her.

His insomnia fueled imaginings of sinister violence that projected relentlessly in his mind like an all-night horror movie marathon. He imagined the worst-case scenarios, but in the end, even his darkest fantasies couldn't assemble the despicable aftermath they were left to sift through. The pain was worse than anything he'd ever felt before or after.

There was a stabbing pain in his heart, prodding his soul when it clicked—he'd done the same thing to Vera. It might not have been the exact same situation, but there were certainly some similarities between the two periods. Daniel just wanted to hold her tight and tell her how sorry he was.

Daniel tried not to think about it anymore, he was just sitting there, sad and sulking. He knew that wasn't what he'd aspired to bring into their home. He no longer wanted to add to the gloom, he aimed to exterminate it. There was no more planning, no more waiting. There was no better time to initiate his metamorphosis than that very instant.

I need to prove myself to both of them. I need to show them that this isn't just some random promise. This is happening. Things are going to change. Things are going to get better. I need to show them that I'm all in. I need to do something to get us on the right path. It needs to be an action, Daniel thought.

He gawked around his disheveled surroundings, looking for something that made sense to him. Something that called to him. His gaze paused on a box of black garbage bags that sat on the kitchen table just a few yards away. That was exactly what he needed to see.

The motivation surged inside him. He wasn't just going to sit around anymore and watch the place rot away. He was going to change the circumstances instead of being a slave to them. He wanted things to be like they were before. He wanted them to be like it was when he used to wait for Vera to arrive home with a giddy childish anticipation.

He used to keep the house in top condition. He used to have a hot meal ready for her. He used to sparkle with a warm love simmering in his eyes when she returned home each day. She didn't have to do a thing. Daniel was ready to make those tender and intimate moments of ecstasy return to them, and he was going to begin immediately.

I'll start with Harold's room. No more garbage, no more shit. I'm going to create a house with standards. If I can do that, hopefully, it'll rub off on the kid. Over time, he'll understand that this isn't any kind of way to live, Daniel thought.

Daniel wheeled his way through the narrow path that was still cleared out enough to squeeze his wheelchair through. He scooped up the plastic garbage bags from the table and laid them on his lap. He then turned himself in the direction of the hallway.

SON OF THE SLOB

As Daniel approached Harold's door, he took notice of the newly installed locking mechanism fixed to the exterior. It was a turn lock, but just the sight of it alone caused a spike of fright to bubble up inside him. He hadn't seen it before, and if Vera had installed it, that could only mean one thing... things had gotten worse.

Move past the fear. It's time for a new way of living, he thought to himself as he reached for the lock.

When the door came open, he wasn't expecting what was on the other side. Harold was still supposed to be in school. He wasn't supposed to be plopped down on the messy floor staring at him with his blank and stoic expression. But regardless, to Daniel, his presence was no longer one to dread. He was going to have to embrace it if this new school of thought he'd developed was to be successful. He pushed the negativity out of his mind and rolled into the raunchy room. He was ready to move forward and set the new standard.

"Harold, I'm sorry I left you, but I'm back now. I'm back for good this time. Things are going to be different. We're going to get back on track again. All this garbage you see will be a distant memory soon," he explained, pulling a black garbage bag from the roll on his lap.

Harold remained both motionless and emotionless. He watched on hypnotically as the bag expanded, and Daniel leaned over to grab a handful of the foul garbage from the mountainous heap beside him.

"Your mom and I cleaned up this place a long time ago. It's been in real bad shape since then, but I promise you, it's going to change. And it starts today," he said, reaching over for another soggy handful of soiled clothing.

Due to the hazardous amounts of mouse and rat droppings alone, never mind the stomach-churning smell, Daniel should have been wearing a mask. But it didn't seem to matter in that moment. The message in the action was more important than breathing in a dusty flurry of crusty vermin waste. It had to change immediately.

Harold watched him without saying a word as Daniel eventually filled the entire bag and then set it off to the side.

"If it's going to get better in here, that's what we have to do to this entire place. It may seem like a lot right now, but I promise, it'll go by quicker than you think. What do you say, son? Will you help me?" he asked, removing another bag from the rectangular box on his lap.

Harold slowly nodded his gnarly head. It was the most interaction Daniel had had with him in some time. It was also the only time that Harold's tiny mind could recall Daniel acknowledging him as his son.

A smile crept across Daniel's face, "That's good, Harold, that's an excellent start. Just do like Dad does and fill up this bag, okay? Then when there's no more room, I'll get you another one."

Harold slowly rose to his feet. His diaper made his pants puff out more than normal. It looked like he had a full load inside because of the squishy sound that trickled off his lower body as he stepped toward Daniel.

Harold took the bag from Daniel and opened it up, just like he'd seen him do moments before. The thoughtless boy felt the plastic against his fingers. The same plastic that his mother used to put the other people inside of.

He thought back to the moments where he'd turned off the other people. When they stopped moving, talking, and breathing. They were so much easier to interact with once they were turned off. Another flash blazed through his mind—the filthy man that had guided him through the whole process. Harold could see him again—he was as real as rain. Sometimes he still heard his voice in his head. Sometimes he still looked for his guidance. After all, there weren't many others that Harold could turn to.

That's where the people go. That's where the people should be. They like it in there. Put him in the bag, the voice inside his skull said.

Harold seemed a bit confused by the direction. He rubbed the sides of his temples, unsure what to make of it. The voice had never misled him before.

SON OF THE SLOB

It's the only place for people. That's why he gave you the bag, he wants you to fill it up. So… fill it up… NOW! the rotten voice screamed.

Harold tremored at the ferocity of the commands. He looked on as Daniel reached for another trash bag so he could continue cleaning. When Harold noticed Daniel take his eye off of him, he pounced.

The next thing Daniel saw was the all-encompassing darkness set upon him. The nothingness that he'd felt trapped in for some time had not only manifested but latched onto him. While he was filled with fright, there was a small sad corner of his being that also embraced it.

Harold pulled back with all of his might as the voice continued. *Keep it on him, he wants it, he needs it.*

The slick plastic interior remained over Daniel's head, and as Harold enthusiastically continued to pull, Daniel's chair tipped backwards.

Once the chair toppled, Harold took the opportunity to mount him while continuing the suffocation. His meaty lower frame descended upon Daniel as Harold sat ass-first on his skull.

While Daniel's arms flailed about desperately, Harold curled his hammy legs around the sides of Daniel's neck, like he was clinging to him for dear life (or death in this case). The smell of Harold's unkept undercarriage easily carried on through both his diaper and the layer of plastic still stretched over Daniel's face.

"That's where people go," Harold muttered.

Daniel punched Harold in the arms and on the sides of his head, but the Son of The Slob remained an immovable object. As the hot fecal air invaded Daniel's nostrils, his oxygen intake was almost non-existent. He was panicking and getting more desperate by the second.

Daniel started to scratch and claw at the sides of Harold's arms, digging into his flesh in desperation. In hopes that the discomfort he inflicted upon him would cause him to move.

But the sets of streaking lacerations that Daniel left running down Harold's biceps and forearms did little to change the course of events. Daniel tried to dig into him even deeper. He could feel the boy's grimy, unbathed skin occupying the space under his fingernails. As he scraped and scratched through layer after layer, more blood continued to crawl down Harold's leaking extremities, but Daniel's efforts did nothing to alter his position.

Daniel's actions began to slow and weaken until they eventually stopped altogether. As the disabled veteran took his final breath, he thought of Vera and all they'd been through. He wished that he'd come home sooner and had the opportunity to tell her how he felt about her one last time. He recalled their first kiss and the slight hint of bubble gum that entered his mouth after Vera removed the wad from between her teeth to plant one on him. But that flavor and memory were snuffed out as he heard Harold begin to defecate again in his already soiled diaper. All Daniel could smell and taste in his final moments was the overwhelming putrid nature of Harold Harlow's neglected body and waste.

Once the fight left Daniel, Harold then released the tension in his hips and rolled sideways off the top of him. He looked back at his stepfather's motionless body for a moment, not sure whether to be in admiration of his sickening accomplishment, or feel a despondency for the departed. His brain was so broken that things he was sure about one minute, could seem like question marks in the next breath.

He shook his husky head from side to side, snapping himself out of the brief stupor. The next picture had inserted itself in his mind already. He didn't know where the ideas came from, but he always liked them.

Harold turned his head forward and crawled over next to the side of his soiled bed. Both of his flabby arms disappeared into the dark space underneath. They returned with a shoebox that had a handful of small holes punched into the sides; there was no intent behind their placement.

Harold cracked the lid slightly and took a peek inside. Beside a small and watery piece of his excrement sat an unnaturally large rat. The diseased vermin was far grander than the other members of the species that had roamed the Harlow house previously.

Its giant ruby eyes were flanked with black fur and a pair of elongated peg-like teeth. The beast looked angry, like it had grown resentful of its time spent in captivity. Like it had a pent-up rage that it was ready to unleash if only it was given the chance to…

Harold stared at the beastly rodent's big blood-toned eyeballs as they glimmered in the room's dim lighting while it reflected back off of them. Harold brandished his bumblebee teeth. He took joy in gazing upon the filthy creature. A stringy droplet of frothy saliva slipped out from the side of his mouth as Harold began to laugh.

MY LOVE NO MORE

The drive home felt like a drag race. I needed to get back to the house and deal with the pair of problems braising in my basement. There couldn't be a more difficult task, but it had to be addressed. The sky was already getting gloomy, but I needed to wait for full-on nightfall before I could delve into activities as dastardly as the ones I had in my queue. The darkness would act as my cover and protection if I was to complete the disposal unnoticed.

There were still many aspects of the dump that I needed to account for, including locating enough weight to ensure they sank to the bottom. The plan wouldn't work if either of the bodies eventually resurfaced. Tina was in pieces, so I would also need to consolidate her into a single sturdy bundle. She was light enough that it shouldn't be a problem. Sister Doomus was another issue.

The weight on my shoulders felt backbreaking, but it could all be lifted with a single short drive. I envisioned myself on the road already. Pulling up to the bridge. Double-checking that the traffic flow around me was as dead as the bodies in my hatch. Muscling the ladies over the gray railing. Watching them crash into the choppy water below. Feeling the relief as they disappeared from my life forever. It would all just seem like a bad dream a short time from now. It would all be over soon.

I reached my driveway before I could finish my morose fantasy. I took a deep breath and said, "You can do this. It's almost over now. Just a few hours away…"

As I reached for the door handle and unlocked it, I exhaled. But no amount of breathing exercises could prepare me for what I would see when I pulled the door open. I was met with a sight that sent me spiraling. All the planning and prioritizing had been for nothing. Instantly, none of it mattered any longer because there was a new crushing problem that I was now faced with. One that was, somehow, of a much more personal and emotional nature.

It appeared that Daniel had decided to return home, but not in the way that I'd hoped. He sat completely still with his wheelchair parked at our cluttered kitchen table. Familiar imagery bombarded me as my mind began to break down and absorb the horrendous scene.

A black garbage bag was tied around my Daniel's head tightly, so much so that I could see the outlines of the face I fell in love with. Flashes of being back in the room that The Slob had confined me to erupted. Sandra was tied to the chair, the trash bag clinging to her face, as she struggled to exist. I could hear her panic-stricken voice in my head, begging me to free her.

I hadn't even had a chance to close the door; the tears started to flow and my flare of hysteria began. "Daniel!" I screamed in a blood-curdling horrified fashion.

He didn't respond to me. Daniel remained statuesque, just sitting, like he was waiting in purgatory.

Unlike Sandra, the movement in Daniel was absent. I didn't know what to do, I was paralyzed. The endless possibilities of how this conclusion had found me stabbed into my head—a surge of mental stress, nearly an overdose-worthy offering.

No matter how I sliced it, the simulated paths all had one common factor—Harold. My disturbed son was nowhere in sight. My blood pumped furiously. *It had to be Harold, who else could it be?*

Then, suddenly, the mouth region of the dark plastic began to move. Maybe it wasn't too late! Maybe there was still some fight left in my soldier after all! He was breathing, Daniel was still breathing!

I ran over to the butcher's block on the left side of the kitchen and retrieved the first knife in my reach. The flick of the steel leaving its wooden holster echoed throughout the room. I had to save him! I couldn't do it without him! There was still time! There was still hope!

I quickly cut into the tough plastic as carefully as I could, but as I expanded the hole, I immediately regretted it. I saw Daniel's eyes first; they were glazed over and void of the slightest sense of fight. They told me all I needed to know, but still, I peeled the bag down further.

As the plastic split open wider, it revealed more of the mystery. I realized that the movement coming underneath wasn't from Daniel breathing. In fact, it wasn't from Daniel at all. It was coming from a massive glob of hairy horror that was currently obstructing his airway. The matted, saliva-soaked mother rat screeched furiously as it scraped, clawed, and bit its way from Daniel's ghoulishly agape mouth.

I tried to scream but my voice box failed to produce any sound. I fell backwards against the filthy wall and slid down to a sitting position. My entire body was tremoring like a carnal earthquake had possessed my being. There would be no glory moment where we reunited. No matter how fiery my love for Daniel was, it no longer mattered. I'd never get to explain it properly again. My daydreams were just that.

I watched on, frozen in repulsion, as the rat maneuvered its massive frame and sunk its fangs deep into Daniel's dead eyeball. As a translucent fluid mixed with the red and gushed down his cheek, I couldn't help but remember what those eyes had meant to me.

The eyes that had only been for me. The eyes of a man that cared more about me than anyone, even himself. The eyes of a man that meant the world to me. The eyes of my only true love.

Suddenly, I shot to my feet, I hadn't even thought about it, the action just came to be. My rage had overtaken my terror and heartache. I was no longer in control of my flesh. I was at the behest of the myriad of emotions that acted as my motivation.

"Leave him alone! Leave him the fuck alone!" I yelled, lunging at the despicable vermin.

I was filled with detestation as I angled the pointed end of the butcher's knife at the fiendish furry. The blade penetrated the hideous rodent's upper body, cutting clean through it and stabbing Daniel's bloody cheek in the same thrust. The rat hissed and cried as its inner workings were unveiled and its lifeblood squirted and sprayed both Daniel and I.

It felt good to hurt it—an insatiable thirst to continue cutting gripped me. I couldn't stop, the overweight creature was still moving, rocking from side to side in Daniel's distorted jaws. I retracted the knife and punctured it again. This time, the cut brought a finality to the beast. I severed its plump head as the gunky blade blasted into the roof of Daniel's mouth. I didn't intend to cut him, but I didn't imagine that he minded any longer. I'm sure he was happy that the rat had met its demise.

The head fell down beside his wheelchair and continued to shake from the nerves in its upper body, while fluid at its neck-stub flooded outward. It was still thrashing about wildly like a machine that had short-circuited. Its pale claws caked in crimson reached outward, asking for help.

I stuck my free hand into Daniel's hellish yawning jowl and pulled the sinister rat's overweight frame from his airway. The blood sputtered hectically like a mini-fountain, drenching most of my face before I dropped the flailing little fuck on the ground beside me.

I raised my heel to the heavens and stomped down with every fiber of my being. The blood that remained in the beast's beefy frame launched out all over the vanilla heating vent that lined the floor of the kitchen.

I stomped on it again… and again… and again…

With each thrust, I felt a measure of relief wash over me. With each bone that splintered and organ that mashed, I felt a further accumulation of bloodlust. I wanted to hurt someone else. I wanted to hurt whoever was responsible for murdering my soulmate.

"That's where the people go," an unmistakable voice muttered from behind me.

I turned my head to see Harold, standing a few yards behind me and grinning ear to ear. He was so fucking happy, but about what? I knew exactly the kind of sadistic hell that would make a blossoming sick fuck like him so joyous. Everything I'd hoped for and believed in was no more. I shouldn't have been surprised.

"HAROLD! WHAT HAVE YOU DONE! WHAT HAVE YOU DONE TO DANIEL!" I shrieked.

The outrage inside me screamed. I was no longer able to defend him. Maybe I shouldn't have in the first place. I had always wanted to give him the benefit of the doubt. He was a victim of circumstance. He was a child of rape. He was not mentally sound. He was born without the most basic human faculties. In advocating for Harold and trying to find the light that laid beyond his darkness, I'd conditioned myself to ignore the most obvious characteristic of who he was as a person: he was evil.

"YOU… YOU FUCKING MONSTER!" I hissed, charging Harold with the bloody knife raised and every intention to use it.

I pounced on him and elevated the knife as high as my arm would extend. I had zero hesitation in aiming for his face. It was so easy to hate him now after what he'd done to Daniel. I wanted to see him come apart. He was able to turn just enough that I clipped his chin and the tip scraped downward, leaving a long slice over his puffy jawline.

I looked at the exposed meat and bone that I'd just unearthed and didn't feel a fucking thing. My brain was static and my senses had gone numb.

When the blood rushed out, it affected Harold strangely; he started to laugh. The same nauseating rows of enamel that I'd tried to call my blood brandished themselves again. But I had finally come to the stark realization that there was no part of me inside him—it was all The Slob. It was everything I'd tried to accept, but in my moment of clarity, I realized, it should have always been unacceptable.

When I pulled the knife back this time, I used my free hand to keep his head in place. He wasn't dodging this one. I couldn't wait until Harold's head came open. I couldn't wait until he was no longer a liability to civilization. With one more swift motion, I'd put an end to the little bastard's depraved legacy. The hurt stopped here, the madness had to end.

But before I could bury the steel in his skull, I heard the subtle patter of footsteps a few feet away from me. The noise was immediately followed by a stern male voice yelling, "Knife! She's got a knife!"

As the pair of bullets entered my body, I felt an intense burning sensation. The suddenness of the shots caught me off guard and left me slumped over sideways. The knife fell out of my bloody shaking hand and scraped across the tile floor in front of me.

My mind began to race but my body felt sluggish. I tried to focus and better understand what was happening to me. I finally gathered enough strength to look up. Through the blurry and surreal imagery that my eyes were digesting, I saw a long navy-blue coat.

Detective Wells stood over me with a horrified look of shock clinging to his scruffy face. A smoking gun rattled in the detective's shuddering hands, and a look of absolute sadness and dejection engrossed him. He wasn't happy about shooting me, that much was clear.

Detective Bates appeared beside him and said, "You had to do it. You had no choice."

"Get the fuckin' phone! Call a medic! Call a medic!" Detective Wells yelled with a disturbed urgency at his equally stupefied counterpart.

"Okay!" Detective Bates replied, rushing over to the phone on the wall.

"Fuck! What the fuck! Kid, are you alright?" Detective Wells asked.

There was no answer, but it didn't really matter because I had stopped listening. My heart was starting to slow and I realized that I didn't need to stay occupied by the detectives scrambling around. As it became more difficult for me to breathe, I realized that I'd wasted a sizable chunk of my last precious moments.

I should have been reliving the handful of magical times in my life, thinking about my family and the better times I'd been privy to by Daniel's side. But I suppose you only die once, and it's hard to know what to expect or how to act when you're in total shock.

I harnessed every shred of passion and strength that remained in my fading body and used it to roll over on my side. I looked at Daniel's mangled face and tried to overshadow the reality with the one I remembered. The one that always had a smile and kiss waiting for me before things got so fucked up.

I had fallen too far away from Daniel to touch him one last time, but I outstretched my bloody hand toward him anyhow. "I'm... sorry," I whispered. "I-I love you."

HOUSE OF HORRORS

Detective Wells stood in the cluttered basement while the crime scene photographer's bulb flashed persistently. He captured the array of disemboweled and crushed rats in addition to the cross outlined in the center of the room, comprised of both knotty and runny fecal matter.

The sacrilegious sight made Detective Wells shudder as he watched the forensic team cut into the numerous black garbage bags. The first one was the largest, and as light was shed on the contents, Detective Wells was not surprised when he saw Sister Doomus's nun garb and lifeless face with a bloody pencil protruding from it.

"Bingo," he mumbled, not happy with the reveal, but also not surprised. "What about the rest of them? Can you cut open a few others?" he asked, noticing that Sister Doomus's body appeared to still be intact.

"What in the holy fuck is in the others?" he whispered to himself nervously.

As the masked forensic team member sliced into one of the other bags, Detective Wells watched his veteran affiliate wince and look away. That was never a good sign.

"I've got a head, couple of arms… Jesus, there's legs in here too," the forensic team personnel said in disbelief.

Detective Wells yelled up the stairs, "Bates! Bates! Get down here! We found her, and at least one more!"

Detective Bates jogged down the steps a few moments later holding a plastic bag in his hand filled with a variety of disturbing Polaroid pictures.

"You're gonna wanna take a look at these too. They found them in her pants upstairs," Detective Bates said, handing the alarming images over to Detective Wells. He looked over at Tina's decapitated head, then over to Sister Doomus's destroyed and shit-caked mug, and finally, down to the dead rats and cross comprised of excrement. "This is why I don't do homicide," he said.

"I don't blame you," Detective Wells replied, removing the lewd pictures from the bag with his gloved hand. "Sorry, I kind of roped you into this one I guess," he added with a grizzled veteran smirk.

"This is… this is fucking disgusting," he said while glancing at a picture of Harold confined in a dark room. It was difficult to tell exactly where the picture was taken— only a stone wall could be seen behind him. The room didn't appear to have any distinguishable items that might clue them in to the location at first glance. That might have been by design.

The first picture depicted Harold down on all fours. He was bent over with the tip of the crucifix, and the head of the man nailed to it, inserted into his anus.

"So, I feel way less bad about shooting this bitch now," Detective Wells confessed, letting out a big huff of stress and anxiety as he spoke.

"You did what you had to," Detective Bates reaffirmed.

Detective wells looked at the inserted crucifix in the picture again, and then back to the disgusting one on the floor near the forensic team.

"Seems like she was some kind of fucking whacked out religious zealot. She sexually abused her son, carved up her disabled husband, killed the nun, hacked up whoever that girl is, and God only knows who else. Would've probably killed the kid too if we didn't show up. But after all this… I'm wondering if he'd have been better off dead…" Detective Wells pondered.

"There's no way he'll ever be normal after an ordeal like this. I'd bet my pension on it," Detective Bates concurred.

"Life is just cycles. I mean, look at this goddamn place, it's literally crawling. It's alive. I've never seen such a level of neglect in my life. I'm surprised the kid is even alive. I can only imagine what kind of diseases he has as a result of living in this fuckin' shithole. Poor bastard's retarded too, there would've been no way for him to escape it. No way to let someone else know what kind of sick shit was going on in here." Detective Wells flipped through the rest of the photos, not really trying to see what they actually offered. He'd seen enough to try and close the case and move on. He slipped them back into the plastic and shook his head.

Detective Bates took them back from him and looked down at the cross created from feces. He joined Detective Wells and shook his head before returning his gaze back to his somber counterpart.

"Upstairs, on the outside of the kid's room, she installed a deadbolt lock and ropes around his bedposts. She must've just kept him trapped inside when she didn't feel like dealing with him. I've seen and heard of some pretty cruel and unusual things in my time, but this… this takes the fucking cake," Detective Bates said with more than a hint of disgust.

"How can someone sink this low? This is the kind of story that you… you can't even explain to someone. They'd have to be here to have any chance of grasping it," Detective Wells replied.

Detective Bates returned his gaze back to the bizarre religious symbolism on the basement floor. "What do you think she was trying to do or say with all this?" he asked, pointing at the blasphemous depiction.

"The two bullets I left in her heart will make sure that question never truly gets answered. I'm not sure it really even matters. Sometimes people are just absolutely fucking crazy. Their brains are broken. The real question is how do they arrive at that moment in time. I can't help but wonder what brought her to this point. This place... it looks like a nightmare to nine out of ten people, but to them, it was just normal."

"It's like you said, after we left the motel, she was shook. Instinct goes a long way. I'm just glad we decided to tail her. It's funny though, I didn't actually expect anything to happen. When we heard the screams, I didn't know what to think. I shouldn't have even been surprised, I shouldn't have underestimated her," Detective Bates replied.

"That's life, I guess. It's just a series of choices. If we didn't act on those feelings and took that one tiny misstep, they'd probably be pulling that fuckin' kid out of the next bag," Detective Wells replied.

Detective Bates tapped his hand nervously against the side of his leg. A chill ran down his spine thinking about the totality of the day's depraved events. He shook it off and looked up at Detective Wells.

"Well, luckily, or maybe unluckily for him... now he'll get another chance."

MORBID CURIOSITY

"You can start with the last time you saw her," Detective Wells said, plopping down in the cushy chair in front of Dr. Plankton's desk like he owned the place.

"Well, she was sitting right there," Dr. Plankton replied, reclining back in his seat.

Detective Wells didn't seem bothered or shocked about the revelation. He just waited for the nerdy man to offer whatever insight he could. He sensed a certain level of apprehension in the Poindexter's posture.

"There is a certain client privilege, a privacy that is supposed to remain intact in these situations. It serves to protect the client, as well as the integrity of the profession," Dr. Plankton continued.

"Vera Harlow is dead, Doc, I don't think it really matters at this point, does it?" Detective Wells countered.

"Well, if it's all the same, it shouldn't really matter to you then either, right?"

He had a point, one that left Detective Wells simmering in an awkward silence. He didn't much care for the snide intelligent types. He didn't tend to get along with them.

"Why are you here exactly, Detective?" Dr. Plankton asked with a shit-eating grin that Detective Wells typically would have been the one to brandish.

"Because I need to know. Call it a... how do they say it? Call it a morbid curiosity. You see the kind of things that I've seen and, after a while, you're just trying to make sense of it all. Trying to remember why you have faith in the human race. Trying to find a reason not to put a gun in your mouth. Trying to figure out the point of all this," he said, swirling his finger around in an all-encompassing manner. His tone sounded totally traumatized and overwhelmed.

"With all due respect, Detective, typically, I charge for this kind of thing," Dr. Plankton replied in a snarky fashion.

"Oh, really? Well, typically, I give people two chances to give me what I want before I start fucking with their lives. You sit back there all high and mighty, but like every other man, you're made of flesh and bone. And if there's anything I've been reminded of over the past few days, it's that the human form is incredibly delicate. It's literally just putty in the hands of society. So, you can be an asshole, but just remember, most assholes always have to look over their shoulder. Is that the kind of life you wanna live, Doc? Or do you wanna give me five minutes of your precious time?"

Dr. Plankton quickly swallowed the lump in his throat, digesting all Detective Wells had explained, and decided to sing. "Alright... what do you want to know?"

"Like I fucking said already, tell me about the last time you saw her," Detective Wells said with a bit of anger now added to his cadence.

"She was a mess. Her husband, Daniel, had just left her. They'd had quite a few issues with her son. Things were incredibly bleak."

"What do you mean her son? You mean their son, don't you?" asked the ever-astute Detective Wells.

"Perhaps, depending on how you look at it."

"Stop speaking in riddles, Doc, just spit it out. Talk to me like I'm an idiot."

A smile crossed Dr. Plankton's face as if to say, 'that shouldn't be too hard.' Clearly, he didn't view the detective as an equal.

"Harold Harlow was a child of rape. I'm sure you noticed the deformities on Vera, you couldn't look her in the eye without acknowledging them."

Detective Wells nodded and waited for him to continue.

"She went through an extremely traumatic experience some years back. One that, quite literally, saw the child that her and Daniel were supposed to be blessed with beaten out of her. Only to be eventually replaced with the seed of her tormentor. So, as you can imagine, those two had quite a few issues to work out. There was plenty of resentment in Harold's mere existence."

"She hated him?"

"Quite the contrary, actually, the resentment wasn't on Vera's part, she was always fighting for him. Trying to fix him. Searching for a silver lining that was really just a ring of rust. It was Daniel that resented him. The whole thing is quite tragic really."

"Why not just get an abortion?"

"It's hard to say. Sometimes when people go through such an extremely traumatic event, they act bizarre, try to deflect the reality of their situation. They sometimes turn into a different person than they were before the incident. In most cases, they're trying to separate themselves from everything they remember. But Vera was different. She embraced the challenge. She sought to highlight the pieces of herself that got muddled in a monster's lineage. She was a special person, regardless of whatever horrible acts you say she committed."

"If you saw what I saw, you might not be saying that."

"Maybe, but I don't think so. I think if you knew what I knew, you'd agree. Honestly, I'm surprised she didn't snap a long time ago." Dr. Plankton spoke of Vera in a way that even he didn't expect. He was caught off guard by the entire fiasco. But he spoke about her like he would miss her.

"I feel even more confused now. Despite the shit she'd been through, you... you make her sound like some kind of saint," Detective Wells said.

"Well, I don't know if you remember or not, Detective, but the devil was an angel too."

WARPED REMEMBRANCES

The followers had flocked to the mass at Saint Leo's. Their attire was dreary and the atmosphere was downtrodden. Father Davenport stood gravely at the microphone, looking first to the closed casket that contained the body of Sister Doomus, and then back at the bewildered crowd that was eager to hear his kind words and absorb the wisdom and all the comfort his heavy heart could offer.

Father Davenport licked his lips and played with his pointed teeth momentarily, before facing the legion of followers that were gathered before him.

"On behalf of the loyal parishioners and families of the church of Saint Leo the Great, I wish to extend our condolences to all who engaged and interacted with Sister Deloris Doomus. We assure you of our prayers and spiritual solidarity in this difficult time. But it's important to ask ourselves, as believers, why we do what we're doing right now. Why is it when one of our own passes from this life to the next that we feel compelled, feel summoned, to gather and offer up our prayers?"

Father Davenport paused for a moment and stroked the side of his face gently. He looked up at the crowd and made eye contact. The group was massive and attentive, hanging on his every word.

"First and foremost, we assemble during the passing of a loved one in order to recall memories. The person, their passion, their moments of grace, their opportunities, which, I think most of you would agree, in the case of Sister Doomus, were few and far between."

Father Davenport looked up from his script again and locked eyes with the crowd. "She had many accolades and proud moments in the sun, but more than anything, she should be remembered for every child that she touched."

The wrinkly priest slyly let one of his hands dip below the wooden podium erected in front of him. His aged cock began to harden as soon as the words with a double meaning left his dribbly old mouth. A rush of blood filled his saggy skin-tube and was further flooded as his veiny hand clamped down on it with all his might.

"Those children that she touched will never forget her," he continued while subtly stroking his misshapen shaft over his religious garb.

From the corner of his glossy eye, Father Davenport gawked at the pair of altar boys kneeling in prayer a short distance away. They had a candid view into the depraved holy man's profile. One that saw the dirty deeds that no one else was privy to. He wanted them to see it. He took comfort in them seeing it.

Their mourning faces attempted to contain their secrets. The pains of silence and suffering that occurred in the shadows, all in the name of religion. They could find no peace. They could speak no evil. They would never escape his wrath.

Father Davenport began to tremble and shake with ecstasy, "Forgive me, th-this is difficult," he explained as his ejaculation erupted in his briefs under the thick robe.

After gathering himself, he mustered the courage to repeat his previous statement once again. "Those children that she touched will never forget her… and neither will I."

THE ENDLESS ORPHAN

A white sedan crept up to the deteriorating gray building with a sign outside that read: King's House of Children. It looked more like a castle than an orphanage. The building itself had holy symbolism fixed to the framework, including an enormous stone cross that sat at the crux of the structure.

The vehicle ventured on through the heavy rainfall and parked in front of the primeval building. The driver's side door popped open. The font plastered on the side panel of the car read: Child Services.

A crisply-dressed man with a well-groomed beard in his early forties exited the car and hurried around to the back. He pulled the black handle and looked into the back seat.

"C'mon, Harold, this place is going to be great. Let's get inside and meet the nice people before we get soaked out here, okay, buddy?" the man asked.

Harold sat absentmindedly in the seat. He looked like he always did; like he'd just had a lobotomy. His hair had grown considerably, he could've been mistaken for a very short in stature man. The nasty scar carved into his flesh, comprised of milky white tissue, wouldn't help to convince anyone that he was a child. He almost looked as if he was just getting out of prison, and in a way, he was, but only to enter a new one.

As the duo raced into the building, the gentleman from Child Services held a folder with some paperwork over his head. He used it to shield himself from the torrential downpour that seemed to almost follow Harold.

Charles King sat awaiting Harold's arrival in the lobby patiently. The interior space looked outdated, like a boy's school from the fifties. It was comprised of antique pieces, not meticulously selected because of their charm, just because they were there.

Charles immediately rose to his feet upon their entry, a smile crawling over his weathered face. He pushed his oversized wireframe glasses up from the tip of his nose toward his brow and removed a fraction of a chocolate bar from his pocket.

"Michael, thanks again for bringing him," Charles said, offering him his free hand.

Michael shook his hand and then handed over the moist folder containing Harold's paperwork.

"Everything's here, he's all yours now," Michael said, nodding his head.

Charles bent over using the hand that was clutching the paperwork to bridge his body. He stretched the other arm out toward Harold and offered him the hearty wedge of delicious chocolate.

"Harold, my name's Charles King, I'll be looking after you moving forward. We're very excited to have you here. I can't tell you just how much we're looking forward to introducing you to the other children. I know you're going to fit right in," he explained.

Harold didn't move a muscle or acknowledge any of the statements or greetings Charles had offered him. He just stared forward, looking into the cobwebbed corner of the dirty lobby. The dirt and filth was something he could relate to. In a twisted way, it made him feel more comfortable than any person ever could or would.

"He's been through a lot, I'm sure he'll warm up real soon though. Right, Harold?" Michael asked with a smile, patting Harold on his back gently.

Harold didn't move a muscle or utter a word. He just continued to stare forward as if he was detached from the slightest semblance of civility.

"Of course, a flower doesn't blossom overnight," Charles concurred, slipping the Hershey bar back into the pocket of his pants.

"Alright then, I guess I will leave you to it," Michael said, once again extending his hand to Charles.

They shook hands and Charles watched as Michael vanished out into the rainfall. He lingered with Harold in the entry a few moments longer until the headlights on the Child Services vehicle lit up. Eventually, the car backed out before disappearing down the long rural driveway and passing the spiky gate at the end.

Once he was sure the car was gone, he looked at Harold and dumped a bucket of ice water on the warm tone he'd previously taken upon their cordial introduction. His pupils darkened and the whites of his eyes narrowed. "Follow me," he commanded.

The pair walked up the chipped stone steps and took a left at the top of the stairs. The hallway was oversized and offered an amount of space that would never be necessary to occupy.

The massive wooden door at the end of the hall looked ominous. The large circular door-pull was plucked from a different era. The atmosphere had a natural edge—it was anything but welcoming. Upon approach, the door required some effort from Charles to finally get it open.

The room beyond was filled with a silent madness. The reveal was a collection of misshapen misfits. Appearing mentally mutant in nature, the caliber of the castaways made it so Harold no longer stood out. He was just another malformed and rejected piece of trash in a landfill of souls who would never be chosen. By the look of the herd, one might have thought that was by design.

"We have a new runt," Charles said, voice booming through the tall ceilings of the room. The deformed children sat on their thin cots staring at Harold with fear in their beady and sorrow-saturated pupils. They knew something that he didn't. They knew what came next. They knew what had to be done.

Charles looked down at the everlasting blankness that was rooted in Harold since the day he was born. The disgust forming inside him caused his lip to curl just before he stared down Harold and said, "From this moment forward, you will refer to me as King! Understood?"

Harold offered no reply. He didn't look at the strange variety of utterly freakish children, or the dreary décor that surrounded him. He just simply continued to exist.

King lifted a blanket up that was folded on the bed beside him. He unfolded it to capacity and then tossed the cloth over Harold's large head.

Immediately, all the other deformed children rushed him. Punches were thrown, kicks were sent, rage was unleashed. They pounded on Harold like a gang on the streets of New York dispatching a rival.

In the darkness under the blanket, Harold felt comfort. The fast-moving limbs that projected toward him from all directions were of little concern. As his bones cracked, skin split, and teeth loosened, he felt comfort. The pain was his only life-long companion.

No matter what, the pain would always be there for Harold. Unlike anything or anyone else, it would never take off in the middle of the night or up and disappear. The pain was simple. It was pure and didn't lie.

After a few more moments of savage violence, King grabbed hold of the blanket and tugged it away. "And make no mistake about it! I am the king of this castle!" he screamed.

The expressions on the surrounding children shifted from a more than healthy fear to wholly unsettled as Harold was once again revealed to them.

He laid on the stone-cold floor with his bulbous nose bent sideways, blood pouring from his nasal cavity, and a pair of fattened lips. As the thick dollops of blood sputtered out from his mouth, he was having trouble catching his breath… because he couldn't stop laughing…

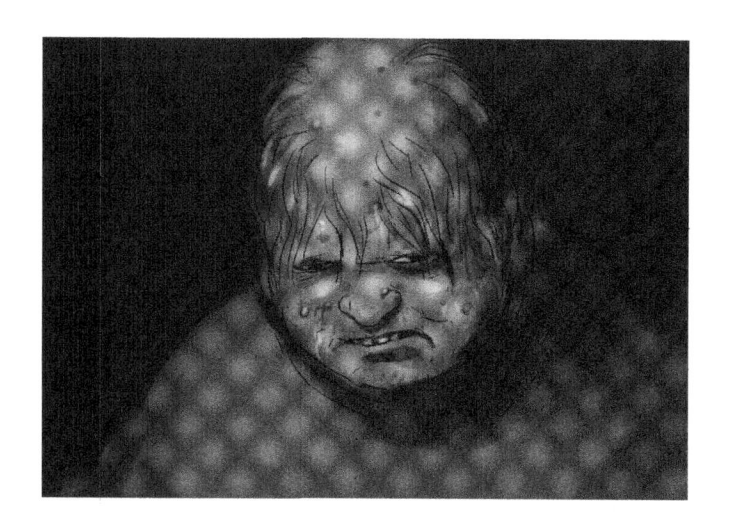

MASS MURDER

Even after eleven years, the church of Saint Leo the Great hadn't changed much. The same entrancing and colorful stain-glass biblical depictions surrounded the worn oak pews. The same seemingly endless arch at the threshold still stretched toward the heavens. The vintage allure and well-maintained statue of a crucified Jesus Christ remained at the altar. But maybe, most unsettling of all, the same people still occupied the church grounds and ran the services.

Father Davenport left some fresh flowers on the altar, still looking lively as ever. His appearance almost seemed eternal, probably because he had leeched the livelihood off of those unfortunate enough to step into his circumference.

He tidied up a bit more before looking at the stairwell to the left of the altar. The church was vacant, it would be hours before the mass started still.

As he descended the staircase, each step was a careful one. He still felt like a spring chicken but his body indicated otherwise. Upon reaching the bottom of the staircase, Father Davenport extracted a red and white spiral of peppermint from his robe.

There was another room that was a bit smaller in the basement, which was used for weekday masses and housed both of the confessional stalls at the rear. They were seldom used as of late—it seemed folks were more comfortable storing their demons than exorcising them.

Father Davenport's mouth salivated as the candy entered it. As usual, he swished it around with his tongue and it clicked and clacked against his thinning yellow teeth.

The smell came out of left field. It was a putrid aroma that wreaked of bodily waste, sweat, and general neglect. As he sniffed around a little further, he realized it was coming from the confession booth. He noticed the partitioning door was closed—a sign that someone had arrived to confess. The potent sensation stung his nostrils and the priest scoffed, shaking his wrinkled head from side to side.

"Animals," he mumbled at an inaudible level.

He didn't want to go in, but he wanted the smell to leave as soon as possible. The sooner he took the confession, the sooner he could breathe again.

When he entered the confessional, the stench only intensified. It made Father Davenport wonder if he could even stick it out long enough to get through the confession. He began to clack the peppermint around in his mouth more rapidly; a subtle sound of protest and distress.

When he looked through the gridded rectangle with the cross inside that allowed a partial view of his follower, he was only further repulsed. Normally, some of the holes were not occupied. Normally, people's physiques weren't so morbidly obese that they nearly blocked out the entire vantage point.

The individual was hairy, the long greasy dandruff dusted follicles were naturally crusted, all but for the patch of balding at the man's crown. The dry skin was raw and peeling. It looked to have ingrown hairs that had developed into sores. A few were filled to capacity with boogery pus, and some had even erupted already and drizzled down his scalp and face like bird shit on a rainy day.

The man's hair and the way his face was angled didn't allow Father Davenport to make eye contact with him. The rows of lard on his acne-scarred puffy cheeks were the only other parts of his face he could see. His flabby front side and discolored shoulders accounted for the rest of the space.

Normally, the parishioner started the confession, but the man inside was making no effort. Father Davenport decided to speak first, determined to expedite the already unpleasant exchange.

"My son," Father Davenport paused momentarily to swivel the peppermint around in his mouth again. "How long has it been since your last confession?"

The man that occupied the booth in front of him said nothing. He just sat there blankly, staring down at the floor below.

"My son… is everything alright?" Father Davenport asked.

The candy continued to click and clack against his jittery teeth as the priest began to feel a bit nervous. The bizarre exchange couldn't end fast enough. He needed to create an out for himself.

"If you're not ready… I-I'm happy to come back later," he explained, reaching for the stall handle.

"Faaatttther," the slurred voice of imbalance began.

"Yes, my son?"

A massive hand suddenly ripped through the venting in the confessional. The punctured wooden separator snapped into pieces, parts of which remained fragmented in the rectangular space.

The hand grabbed onto Father Davenport's pointy nose and didn't let go. He screamed as the powerful mitt pulled him through the newly fashioned space.

As his head and neck entered the splintery window, the jagged wood carved into his tender furrowed flesh. The surface wounds left the priest's head stuck through the other side of the stall as Father Davenport bellowed out the raging terror in his torso.

Just before the hand's meaty thumb went into his left eye, he saw a face that felt like it was from another lifetime. One that he'd long forgotten amid the army of other casualties he'd left on his path of perverse excess. The horrifying face of Harold Harlow.

While Harold might have remained an afterthought to the wicked leader, Harold hadn't forgotten about the wolf in sheep's clothing. There weren't many things that Harold's brain could do right anymore, but somehow, he never forgot. Every fucked-up moment he'd found himself ensnared in was all still accessible.

Father Davenport didn't need to look for the evidence, it was erupting out of his eye socket as Harold's digit dug inside deep enough to reach his thumb's knuckle.

The screams were like music to Harold's ears as he hooked his thumb upward and used it to elevate Father Davenport's head.

The old man closed his drooling mouth as a casserole of clumpy coagulated blood and fluid cascaded down his cheek. In his moment of anguish, he began to thrust the peppermint around in his mouth over and over, trying to calm himself however he could.

Harold grinned, brandishing his tartar encrusted enamel like he was having a perfect day. He then thrust his porky palm into Father Davenport's mouth. His long, tarnished fingernails burrowed into the priest's slimy mouth muscle. He grabbed hold of the back area of the tongue and pulled with all his strength.

The ripping noise sounded like a piece of paper at first and, eventually, a wet kiss. As the pulsating pink detached from his oral cavity, the blood filled the old man's mouth and spewed out all over both Harold's lap and the floor of the booth. It looked like a human garden hose of gore as it continued to burst outward. It was like the blood knew it should have been shed a long time ago.

As Harold handled the ripped-off tongue, it squirmed in his wide palm like a worm on fire. The piece of the depraved priest that was most effective had been taken from him. The piece that he used to groom, sweet-talk, and convince his flock that he was setting an example. The piece of him that allowed him to be a god in the shadows.

Harold kept Father Davenport's face elevated by fish-hooking his eye hole still and looked him in his lone peeper.

"You lie," Harold said, showing off his increase in vocabulary.

Harold put the squirming bloody muscle into his mouth and let his blackened teeth crush down on it. He ground them back and forth, but it took a few moments before he was able to properly tenderize the gamey meat and swallow Father Davenport's most effective tool.

The old man was severely damaged, the shock had his heart racing violently, he felt as if it might explode any second. The agony was so profound that, in his mind, he prayed and begged for his heart to fail. But God had a different vision of his fate.

Harold's sharp nails dug into his fragile neck next. It had already been gashed open by the fragmented wood of the vent, so he inserted them in the hole that was already open and calling to him.

He removed his left thumb from the priest's ruby eye socket and embedded it on the other side of his throat. Harold's eye's widened and he looked into the priest, he could see the darkness inside him. He was feeding off of it. He continued to dig in and burrow further until he could feel even more muscle and bone.

He watched Father Davenport gag and choke but that didn't halt his progression. Once he had reached a depth inside where he felt comfortable, Harold paused and tightened up. He looked into his eyes one final time and pulled back as hard as he could.

***

The rows began to fill with a steady stream of parishioners in the main upstairs church. They slowly filed in amid the calming sounds of the church organ, ready to begin another trying and tiresome week. The attendance was as good as ever, there was hardly any room left on the pews as the service grew ready to blossom.

The choir of kind elderly ladies sang sweet hymns of salvation, positivity, and perseverance, while the churchgoers quietly chatted amongst themselves. But as the clock rolled a few minutes past 7:00 PM, the loyal audience began to get a bit uncomfortable. The polite conversation evolved into grumbles of impatience.

Never being a man to miss a sermon, Sister May and the other ladies seemed a bit confused by the absence of Father Davenport. None of them had seen him in the last few hours but still had faith that he would arrive regardless.

The altar boys were in position, kneeling a short distance away from the podium that should soon be graced with the presence of Father Davenport.

Everything seemed quite ordinary outside from his absence until one of the altar boys took notice of the dark robe that Father Davenport typically donned draped over the podium. It was as if he'd left it there to use the bathroom and would be returning to recollect it any moment.

But as the minutes carried on, it seemed less and less likely. The smaller blonde boy of the pair noticed that the robe was slightly distorted—it appeared different than if the cloth had just been laid there to rest. Like something was underneath it.

As the moans of the followers continued to elevate, the nuns remained in place. They weren't quite sure what to do next. They had never required a back-up plan.

Curiosity got the better of the bony blonde altar boy as he made the sign of the cross and rose to his feet. It only took him a few steps to get within arm's length of the podium and Father Davenport's robe.

But as he drew closer, he noticed something—the dark color of the robe looked somewhat abnormal. It appeared wet to the touch. Something inside him continued to pilot him forward. He didn't know why he did it, but he plucked the robe off of the podium and cast it aside.

Immediately, the entire room roared with a horror so deafening that if God didn't hear it, then he didn't exist. Underneath, in a pool of blood, sat Father Davenport's mutilated head. The deformities and crushing death that Harold had inflicted upon him on display for the masses. His tongue-less mouth left agape as if he still wanted to say something, but he could say no more.

The young blonde boy didn't seem initially affected by the gruesome sight. The priest's destroyed head was a representation of horror for most, but to the altar boy, it had an entirely different meaning. The boy calmly tilted his head to the side and squinted his baby-blue eyes at the monstrous lump of death. On Father Davenport's forehead, there was a single word written in blood: LYAR.

The altar boy exhaled deeply, releasing many emotions at once. They were emotions that no one else would ever know were trapped inside him. A darkness and depression that can't just be shared in passing.

He turned back to the seated members of the audience who remained stunned and screaming, and processed the fright and repulsion on their faces. He couldn't relate. Suddenly, the boy allowed a grin to discreetly crease the side of his mouth. It was the first time he'd smiled in months.

ABOUT THE AUTHOR

Aron Beauregard is the author of the Splatterpunk Award-Nominated book "The Slob." Additionally, he's written a buttload of other books. He still really likes onions regardless of the government smear campaign. He farts in elevators when he's alone and tries to "smell it all up" for himself before the next person enters, as not to offend. He is seen as "just a guy" but often donates to charities that promote spread of disease and harmful ideas. He once worked at a shopping mall where all he and his goonish friends did was get high in the back and sell drugs out of the store, to the chagrin of the mall manager. Somehow, he became a writer and podcaster but he's largely a useless wad of humanity.

MORRIS

COMING SOON?

Printed in Great Britain
by Amazon